WRAP IT UP!

WRAP IT UP!

WELCOME TO LILY ROCK HOLIDAY MYSTERY
BOOK 3

BONNIE HARDY

ON THE OTHER HAND BOOKS

For a full list please go to

bonniehardywrites.com/Books

Welcome to Lily Rock Holiday Mystery Novellas

'Tis the Season *

All Aboard for Murder *

Wrap it Up! *

Lily Rock Mystery Series

Getaway Death *

Influenced to Death *

Deadly Admission *

A Thymely Death *

Deadbeat Dad *

A Very Tidy Death *

Sit. Stay. Play Dead

Redondo and Rose Neighbors in Crime

A Doula to Die For *

Between the Sheets *

Sight Unseen *

Class Dismissed

"Christmas isn't just a day. It's a frame of mind."

Valentine Davies "Miracle on 34th Street"

CONTENTS

GET A FREE SHORT STORY

Join my newsletter to get the latest news about the Lily Rock Mystery Series, Welcome to Lily Rock Holiday Novella Series, and the Redondo and Rose Neighbors in Crime Series.

Along with contests, discounts, giveaways, and events, I'll send you *Meadow's Hat,* a free short story download. Signup on bonniehardywrites.com/newsletter

ELF TWO RETURNS

MEADOW MCCLOUD

"I don't get it." Avery Denning stood next to Meadow's elbow. She'd been called over to the pony corral while they waited for the police to arrive. "Who'd want to off a clown, for gosh sake? They're harmless. Unless, of course, you have some kind of phobia. I guess that might be a good reason." She kicked at the dirt with her elf boot.

Since the year before, everyone in Lily Rock affectionately called Avery Elf Two. Returning for another Christmas in Lily Rock, she'd agreed to wear her costume again while assisting Meadow with the Christmas wrapping station. It had taken a bit of persuasion on Meadow's part to get her to commit.

"So Logan's still coming?" Avery asked. Logan had been Elf One to her Elf Two the year before.

"He said he'd come," Meadow assured her. "I really could use your help, dear."

Hopefully they'll bring the necessary enthusiasm for this project. I am very busy and not in the mood this year. I can't wait until January when I put all the decorations away.

Instead of sharing her fatigue and her lack of Christmas

spirit, Meadow had made every effort to act as chipper as usual. Talking to Avery included. She explained in effusive detail, "The library could make a lot of cash through the wrapping center. Lily Rock shoppers love to buy gifts, then drop them off for wrapping and pick them up later. Very good for small town retail."

She took a breath and continued, "Shoppers often donate more than is necessary because of the good cause. All the proceeds go to the Friends of the Lily Rock Library."

When Avery didn't readily commit, Meadow took a deep breath and kept talking. "Plus everyone remembers you as the elf who saved Christmas last year."

She paused, giving Avery a chance before launching into her next bit of encouragement. Finally Avery sighed and asked, "What about Maguire?"

"You mean Mayor Maguire," Meadow corrected. "Now that he has an official title, he isn't being chased by animal control. He'll be there like usual. I suspect the mayor will love a good wrapping station. Especially when he can shake a paw and collect a dog treat when shoppers drop off and pick up their packages."

"Okay then," she finally said. "I'm in. I can't resist that mutt. And now that he has influence with the Old Rockers and the town council, he'd be good to have as a reference." Meadow smiled at Avery's teasing tone.

Standing next to her this morning, Meadow felt proud of Elf Two. For two years in a row she'd been left behind by her family at the holidays. They had other things to do, like skiing in Switzerland with their friends. But instead of feeling sad, Avery had been applying to colleges and using her time wisely. As a senior at the Lily Rock Music Academy, she had a good chance of getting into an excellent school.

Meadow shrugged. "I planned on helping you set up the wrapping station. This is the week before Christmas. But maybe we should delay until the police arrive. I don't want to leave all of those frightened ponies with only two men to handle them."

"You mean one man and a drunk," Avery mumbled, referring to Thornton, who sat on the bench outside the barn with his eyes closed, his chin dropped to his chest.

"Don't call him that, dear," Meadow gently reprimanded her. "He's had a terrible year, what with his wife in jail. It only added to his drinking issues. I know. I've been there. He needs our compassion."

Avery glanced at Meadow. "I didn't realize. You're an alcoholic?" She sounded perplexed.

"A recovering alcoholic. With Sage's help, I've been sober for fifteen months. I know what Thornton's going through. He's self-medicating. I did tell the doc, but he's not been able to assist. At least not yet."

"Sorry," Avery mumbled. "I didn't know."

"That's okay, dear. No one would expect you to be aware of my problems." Meadow glanced toward the corral. Justin held the agitated pony's bridle, petting her nose, Baubles the clown still slumped against her front leg.

"Who's the tall, skinny guy?" Avery asked.

"That's Justin Young. The doc hired him to care for the ponies and horses at Paws and Pines. He helped at the shelter and with Baubles's act. I'm going over to have a word."

"And get closer to the dead clown?" Avery sounded incredulous.

Meadow looked at her more closely. "Are you one of those people who, you know, is fearful of clowns?"

Avery made a circle in the dirt with the toe of her elf boot. "Kind of," she whispered. "They creep me out."

"How about this?" Meadow said kindly. "Why don't you wait on that bench while I check on Justin and the pony? I also want to see what's keeping Officer Jets, she seems to be taking a long time getting here. Her office is only across the street. But as soon as she arrives, I'll head back to the library. Maybe by then Logan will be here."

Avery looked relieved. Then Meadow pointed and said, "Oh look! There's Logan now. You two can wait together."

Avery's fearful expression was replaced by a wide-eyed appraisal of the young man approaching. "Whoa," she muttered. "Are you sure that's Elf One?"

Watching Logan saunter across the path toward them, Meadow had to admit that since he'd switched schools and gone down the hill for his last year in high school, he'd changed quite a bit. "He's grown," she said. "At least three inches taller."

"He's not even fat anymore." Avery did not disguise the admiration in her voice. "And he's been working out. Look at those shoulders."

"And look at his grin. He seems quite sure of himself, not at all like last year."

Avery half-turned toward Meadow. "Come on. No one changes that much. He's still a geek and a pain." A flush rose to her cheeks.

"Are you blushing, dear?" Meadow asked innocently.

"Not likely," Avery scoffed.

Meadow shrugged. "Okay then, I'll leave you two to catch up while I wait with Justin for Janis Jets to arrive."

"You're braver than I ever could be," Avery stated. "Clowns are really creepy."

BAUBLES AND SPARKLES
MEADOW MCCLOUD

"Don't come any closer," Justin warned Meadow. He patted the pony's neck. "I'm trying to keep Sparkles calm until the cops get here."

"I can see that." Meadow held out her hand for the pony to nuzzle. "Do you think she knows that Baubles is unconscious?" Meadow wanted to add *and most likely dead*, but she didn't. She knew from past experience that Janis Jets and the paramedics preferred to determine who was actually dead and who wasn't.

Justin's voice sounded clouded with emotion. "They were quite the act, Baubles and Sparkles. Shetlands are such great animals. And she's a beauty. Look at that mane and tail. Thick and glossy. Plus she's a palomino. I wonder where she'll go, now that he's gone."

The pony raised her head, eyes focused on Justin. She let out a loud whinny. "It's okay, Sparkles. You're in safe hands." Meadow used her most soothing voice.

The horse shifted her weight, leaning closer. Meadow drew nearer to get a better look at the clown slouched in front of the pony. She'd never seen Baubles out of his costume. She wasn't sure if she would have recognized him without the face paint and red wig.

He dressed as what they called a personality clown. Meadow had been assigned by the Old Rockers to research him online before they hired him. She had done the check quickly, but she didn't find anything unusual. So she gave him a thumbs-up right away.

Her search had revealed photos and videos of Baubles at birthday parties. He used his lasso to do cowboy tricks, and one of his gags was to let children honk his big red nose. He also included a lot of running and falling and begging for attention in his act, which never failed to draw laughter.

The children loved him. Even adults enjoyed Baubles. Especially when he'd drop everything as one of his gags. He juggled balls in the air which fell to the ground one by one. While people were pointing, Baubles would take a drink from their hand and give back the empty container. He'd raise his lasso and circle it around his head, only to miss his target. Several attempts had to be made before the rope landed where it was intended—over a child who giggled at the fun.

But today he didn't look anything like his online presence. *Is it still impolite to stare if the person is dead?* Meadow wondered.

And then on cue, the clown's body began to sag. First a shoulder slumped, and then his entire body drifted to the side. His head hit the ground with a thud.

Sparkles skittered and whinnied. She pranced away from the body. Her distressed neigh pierced the air. She nearly stepped on the clown's hand before rearing back again.

Meadow stepped aside to allow Justin a chance to calm the pony. She shook her head, feeling out of her element. Then she shuddered. *Maybe I should call Sage for some help. She's very good with horses and ponies.*

3

HANGING PICTURES

SAGE MCCLOUD

"Here's the last box," the man muttered. He wore a T-shirt that read "Movers not Shakers." Sage McCloud had contacted him last minute, on the off chance he'd drive up the hill to help her out.

"I paid through Venmo," Sage called after him.

"Yeah. We're settled. Hope you have a good winter break unpacking. Good luck." He was out the door with his dolly. She avoided looking at the unopened boxes and instead glanced around her office.

Her eyes took in the expanse of wall behind her desk and then returned to the stack of papers sitting in the middle. Student applications needed to be read before the end of her holiday. Otherwise she'd miss a deadline and be behind.

Sage wanted to convince the town council that she'd been a good hire. They'd gone out on a limb for her, after all. The youngest director and principal ever in the history of the school.

"I majored in music composition," she'd told the interviewing committee. "But I think I can be the principal. I was born and raised in Lily Rock. I know how music students work, being one myself. And I can connect the boarding students with the rest of the community. It will lessen the homesickness and bring a bit of life back to the town."

She'd gotten the call an hour after the interview. Of course it didn't hurt that her mother, Meadow McCloud, ran Lily Rock from her desk at the library. She'd done that for years, what with her connections as an Old Rocker.

Meadow would explain to anyone who asked, "Old Rockers are residents who've lived here a long time. Decades count in Lily Rock. You can't dismiss our collective wisdom."

Sage knew her appointment, as the director and principal of the music academy, was an attempt by the Old Rockers to keep things just like they used to be. With the possible exception of attracting more qualified students, which they hoped she'd be able to do, considering her background and younger age.

With a hammer and a picture hanger, Sage took one framed photo out of the box. She tapped the nail into the wall and hung the photo, stepping back to smile. "Mom and me," she announced to the room.

Meadow wore her customary blue denim jumper, her hair in a long braid that hung over her left shoulder. Sage wore a crimson sweatshirt and a cap. USC was boldly printed in gold letters over the bill. *I was so eager in those days.*

Both the women wore big smiles.

Sage mused. *Mom was sure proud of me when I finally got accepted. I was the oldest in my class, but I didn't let it stop me.* She remembered how one professor complimented her on how smoothly she'd handled the age difference.

"You're more like faculty than a student," Dr. Marrs had

said. It had taken Sage nearly a decade to apply for college. She didn't want to leave Lily Rock or her mom. But after that, Dr. Marrs became her mentor. He was the first she told about her new job. He'd taken her to lunch to celebrate. "Good luck in Lily Rock, Sage. You're the only student who's leaving with a job already in her back pocket."

She'd packed all her belongings and returned to Meadow's house. At first it felt cramped. Meadow had a tendency to put her nose into Sage's business. But once they'd established a few boundaries, things went much more smoothly.

The next photo, placed to the side of the first, was of Sage on a horse with a handsome man holding the bridle. "Gosh, Doc looks young," she commented, straightening the frame. He'd been her surrogate dad for as long as she could remember. Teaching her how to ride on her first pony at the age of four. When she got older she spent hours at Paws and Pines exercising the horses.

Once Sage had arranged the photos, she began to install musical instrument wall hangers. First she hung a five-string fiddle, made for her by a luthier in Colorado. He'd given it to her as a gift after a great summer of making music in the mountains.

And then an old fiddle without strings. Rumor had it that Mother Maybelle Carter had played that very fiddle in the '50s. Sage had been unable to confirm that rumor, but she appreciated the used look of the old instrument. *I need to buy some new strings.* Sage grabbed a scrap of paper to start a list.

She had only one more instrument to go. Digging deeply into the box, a musty smell made her sneeze. "Achoo!" She rubbed her nose. *Must have brought in some pollen.* She pulled up the wooden box with five angles. One was much shorter than the other, giving an overall impression of a triangular shape.

A series of pegs lined two of the straight edges. Broken strings looked rusty. She ran her finger over the metal casings, feeling layers of corrosion. *This will be so hard to fix. I've got to buy new strings. On the list they go.*

She turned the instrument over, running her hand across the wood surface. Dust lifted from the instrument, filling her nostrils, bringing up another sneeze.

"Did you mug a kindergarten teacher?" came a voice from the doorway.

Brad May grinned at her, looking laid back as ever. His jeans, slung low on his hips, accompanied a maroon hoodie. He'd dressed that way for years, even after graduating from high school.

"I found it at a garage sale," she told him. "It called to me for some reason. I don't know anyone who plays autoharp anymore." She looked at the wall. "But it will make a good ornament for my wall."

Brad frowned. "Anyone who plays that thing has to be old."

"Don't be ageist," Sage said, dismissing his assessment. "Help me out here. I want to hang it right there." She drilled the instrument hanger into the wall. Brad helped her adjust the fit.

Rubbing the back of her hand over her forehead, Sage sighed. "That should do it for now. I've unpacked all the boxes." She turned to Brad. "So to what do I owe this pleasure?" The smell of weed wafted off of Brad's shirt.

"Ah yeah, I guess I did come here with a message." Brad scratched his head. "She's been trying to call you. Meadow. I came right over to deliver the news in person."

"What's wrong?" Sage lifted her phone off the desk. "I've

been so busy I haven't looked at my phone." She found two missed calls and three texts. "Is there a problem?"

Sage remembered that only recently she'd been impatient with Meadow's constant texting and she'd called her out. "This thing," she'd held the cell in the air, "feels like an umbilical cord. The way you keep texting and calling. Kind of desperate. I'm not a baby anymore. You don't need to know my every move."

Before Meadow could disagree, Sage added, "I want to move back home, Mom, but not if you keep tabs on me every single second."

Then Meadow's face had gone white. A look of fear crossed her eyes. "You're right, dear. I will stop. But just in case of an emergency..."

Sage now held her cell in her hand. This was the first time Meadow had broken her commitment to not keep texting and calling. "What's the matter? Or is this just another check-in by Meadow?"

"She's in a bit of a situation," Brad explained. "A big commotion at the pony corral in town. They're waiting for Janis Jets. Thornton found a dead body at the pony ride. Maybe you could come down and keep Meadow company while she waits."

Sage reached for her keys and then skirted past Brad toward the door.

4

―――――

"HE'S A GONER"

SAGE MCCLOUD

Though it was still early morning, the Lily Rock streets were lined with holiday shoppers. Cars honked, people ambled across the middle of the road blocking traffic. There was no parking place to be found.

Sage finally gave up and edged her truck down an alley. She found a spot behind the library next to a dumpster. She turned the ignition key, her hand shaking. *I hope Mom is okay.*

She rushed across the street into the park toward the corral. A tall man standing at the edge of the path called out, "Hi, Sage."

his broad shoulders filled out a blue flannel shirt. When he smiled, she immediately felt less anxious. "Mike, can you tell me what's going on?"

Dark blue eyes clouded over. "Baubles was found dead," he explained. "Your mom is helping with his pony while they wait for the paramedics to deal with the body and the police to arrive."

Sage's anxiety returned at his words. "Did my mom find

the body?" Before he could answer, she ran toward the corral.

He grabbed her arm, forcing her to stop. "I'd stay out of that scramble if I were you. No one wants to move anything until Janis arrives. Which means they don't need anyone to enter the crime scene. Plus Janis would have to give the okay first."

Michael Bellemare, Lily Rock's famous architect, knew what he was talking about. He'd come to know Officer Jets's routine from past experience.

Sage took a deep breath. Instead of rushing away, she leaned into Michael's shoulder for support. "Makes sense," she said. "So long as you think Meadow's okay."

"I think she's just fine. In her element, to be honest. Right at the center of all the action." He grinned sheepishly and then added, "I don't have to tell you."

As her only child, Sage was quite used to Meadow's nosy ways. Especially during holiday events when Meadow took on the decorating and celebrating with a vengeance.

It was Meadow who organized the Lily Rock tree lighting and the nativity display every year. By the time the week before Christmas rolled around, she made everyone just a little crazy with her joy and expectations, along with giving orders.

Her mother would barely sleep on Christmas Eve, preparing the dough for the cinnamon rolls and the ham and the rest of the side dishes for her day-long open house. "It's tradition!" she'd tell those who asked.

Satisfied that her mother was all right, Sage viewed the rest of the people lingering near the corral. Her eyes stopped on two familiar teens. "Elf One and Elf Two." She nudged Michael.

"Yep, they're back." He grinned. "We must have been

pretty successful last year, keeping them from feeling sorry for themselves. I guess Meadow contacted them and did some convincing. She needed volunteers for her gift-wrapping fundraiser. They both agreed."

"I ran into Avery at Thanksgiving. She told me that she and Logan kept in touch with the occasional text. Since his parents pulled him out of the academy after the incident at Old Toy Trains." Sage looked toward the building they called The Fort.

Designed like something out of a frontier town, a variety of retail shops filled the two-story structure, including tarot readers and a beef jerky specialty booth. "It looks naked without that old nutcracker," Sage said.

"No one misses that thing," Michael insisted. "But the new toy store is certainly less flamboyant."

The upstairs shops could be accessed by a set of outdoor stairs. A boardwalk circled the building. Boughs of greenery hung on railings. Each shop window displayed extravagant hand-tied red bows along with fairy lights and decorative ornaments.

"Didn't Baubles have his own Bauble-themed ornament this year?" Sage asked. "That's kind of sad. If he's dead and all."

"Very sad," Michael agreed. "He became popular really fast with the children. It felt like he'd lived in Lily Rock forever."

"I wouldn't recognize Baubles on the street without his costume," Sage admitted.

"Me neither," Michael agreed. "He certainly took his persona seriously. Never appeared in public without the clown face and big red nose. The kids loved honking it. And he was so patient. He'd lean over and as soon as they'd honk, he'd fall over dead."

"Oh God, that's true. And now he really—probably is—dead." Sage's stricken face brought a smile to Michael's lips.

"Too soon?" he asked.

"Definitely too soon. At least until we find out what happened," Sage admitted.

"So since Janis isn't here yet, why don't the two of us make our way through the crowd. It's taking so long, maybe your mom would feel better if she caught sight of you about now."

Sage didn't need another invitation. She tried squeezing her way around a man standing in front of them, but when he didn't budge, Michael announced in a loud voice, "Excuse me." When the man still didn't move, Michael ducked around, leading with his elbow, and made his way in front of him. Michael turned his head. "Police business," he explained, taking Sage's hand.

On the way to the corral, Sage assessed the situation. "Let's say hi to Mom and then gather up the rest of the Shetlands. They're probably done for today and getting more nervous just standing around."

"Most likely," Michael agreed. "But Janis may want to have a look at them when she gets here. They are evidence. Witnesses, if you think about it."

"You just assume there's been a murder?" Sage hoped it had been a heart attack or something health-related and unexpected.

"I don't have to assume." Michael pointed toward the pony circle. "Take a look for yourself."

Sage stopped in her tracks. Meadow held the head of the agitated Sparkles close to her chest. She whispered into the pony's ear, staring down at the clown's body, face planted in the dirt.

"I know exactly what she's saying," Sage said. "Mom is

telling him what she always told me whenever I was upset. 'Don't look back. You're not going in that direction.'"

"Really?" Michael's eyebrows raised. "That's a funny thing to tell a kid or a pony. She really said that?"

"Ever since I can remember," Sage affirmed. "I always thought she had something in her past she couldn't quite make peace with. So she put on a happy face and just moved forward."

Michael pointed to the ground near Meadow and the pony. "That must be Baubles. Geez, there's a rope around his neck. Probably is a murder then."

"That's his clown prop. He'd do tricks with the rope and then lasso a child and pull them closer to give them a piece of candy. How awful. To be strangled by your own prop."

"We don't know for sure that's what happened," Michael warned. Sage was about to retort when a voice interrupted.

"Not until I say that's what happened." Janis Jets stood next to Michael's elbow. She wore a grim expression, and her navy blazer covered the familiar bulge at her waist—the indication that she was carrying her weapon. Hair tied back in a bun, she seemed ready for action. "How's it going, Mike?" she asked.

He shook his head. "It's difficult to see with so many people standing around," he explained.

"A good thing too. Don't need you two in the middle of my crime scene." Jets's voice held no room for doubt.

"You've already looked at him?" Michael asked.

"Come on, you're a smart guy. I don't have to get any closer. You can see for yourself, even from here, that's one dead clown. He's a goner." Jets made her way forward, shoving people out of her way. Then she turned back. "Okay, you can come. I need someone to be with Meadow."

5

A HORSE IS NOT A PONY

Sage McCloud

Sage wrapped her arms around her mother. She leaned in to speak in her ear. "I'm so sorry I didn't get here sooner. I was unpacking and didn't check my phone. And then the crowd!"

Meadow leaned back from her embrace. "Do you have a tissue, dear?"

Reaching into her pocket, Sage pulled out a small packet. "Just like you always told me. I'm prepared."

Meadow dabbed at her nose, forcing a smile. "Do as I say, not as I do. I didn't have any tissues when I left the house."

Without Meadow's reassuring attention, Sparkles began to nose at Sage's shoulder. "It's okay, girl." Sage took her bridle. "We'll get you back to the barn."

Growing up with horses, Sage knew to look Sparkles in the eye. What she saw there was disturbing. *The pony's terrified. And has maybe lost her trust.* A tall man sauntered closer to them. His worn jeans and dusty cowboy boots were a giveaway. *He works with horses,* Sage concluded.

"Do you know Justin?" Meadow asked. "Doc hired him as a wrangler over the holidays. He works at Paws and Pines."

Sage nodded in the man's direction. While Meadow continued to explain, "He was here quickly, right after the body was...found." Meadow's voice grew soft.

"Hey, Justin," Sage finally said. "I'm Meadow's daughter, Sage."

"Hello," he said. His haggard face and puffy eyes made Sage wonder when he'd last gotten any sleep.

Justin began to explain. "I don't know what I'd have done without Meadow's help. Once I found Baubles," he paused, "everything broke loose. The ponies got restless. I thought maybe they'd make a break for it."

He used his finger to swipe in front of his neck. "I didn't see the rope right away. I figured Baubles had a heart attack or something."

"No more of that speculation. The professionals will take it from here." Janis Jets came closer, apparently having caught the tail end of the conversation. She reached out to pat Sparkles. The pony snorted and struck out with her back hoof, nailing Janis right in the knee.

"Stop that!" Jets jumped back. She rubbed at her knee through the tan slacks. "I thought small horses were nicer than the big ones."

"She's a Shetland pony," Justin explained. "You can't approach a big animal that way. Not even ponies. Especially if you don't know them. Here, let me show you." Justin took his hand and ran it along Sparkles's neck, over the saddle, toward her flank. He stood close to her body.

Once he got to her rear, he didn't drop his hand but walked around her tail, still touching her back haunch. He didn't lift his hand until he'd made a full circle.

"Use your hand so she knows you're in charge but mean her no harm. Keep your body close to hers so she can't lift that leg and give you a kick." Justin looked up at Janis.

"I'm not trying to be all horsey here," Janis grumbled. "I leave that up to you Paws and Pines people. I'll call my guy to look over Miss Sparkles for evidence. And then get this undersized horse out of here. I can't have her injuring anyone else." She rubbed her knee again with a scowl.

"Sparkles would like nothing better," Justin sniffed. "Get some ice for that as soon as you can." He pointed to her leg.

Jets ignored him. She walked away toward a paramedic standing near a freshly installed crime tape. "I know you're not a vet, but take some snaps of this pony for forensics. We need to get all of these animals back to the barn." She waved her hand toward the corral.

"What about all of that?" The paramedic gestured at the festive Christmas ribbons braided into Sparkles's mane and tail.

"Yah, have a look. But be careful. She kicks. Now get going." Jets limped back to the corral toward Sage. This time Jets shifted her attention to Baubles the clown. He'd been covered with a mylar blanket. She lifted the blanket to look at his face, peering more closely to take in the rest of his body. "Such a short guy. Made a good clown though. The kids loved him. One rope trick too many. Very sad."

Sage held her breath as Janis's hand lingered close to Baubles's fake nose. *Oh no, she wouldn't...she couldn't...* To her relief, Janis covered the body with no further comment, failing to honk the clown's nose.

"Okay then," Jets growled. "Baubles is dead. I don't know

what the medical examiners will tell us, but from my perspective he's been strangled. The rope is a pretty obvious clue."

"Who would want to kill Baubles?" Meadow's voice cracked. "And so close to Christmas too."

Jets turned to her. "Did you know him well?"

"I hired him. For the town council. We did some planning together for the holiday season." Meadow sniffed.

Sage reached for her hand. "It's okay, Mom," she said softly.

"Maybe okay for the rest of you," Jets huffed. "You can go back to eating red and green cookies and putting icicles on your fake trees. But not for me. I have to report this death and get into my investigation as soon as possible." She looked around the remainder of the crowd.

"Any one of these people could be our killer."

"Probably not," Meadow said. "None of them were here when Thorny found the body. I came right away. Then Brad arrived. Finally Justin turned up. The crowd gathered long after that. Because you took so long to get here," she added.

"I'll have you know I had important business to attend to." Jets's mouth drew a straight line. She pulled out her cell. "So you said you discovered the body at 6:30 a.m. I didn't get a call until nearly an hour later."

"Thorny must have been in shock. That's why he didn't call. Imagine being the one to find a clown slouched against a horse with a rope around his neck. That's horrifying for anyone."

"And what about you? Aren't you part of this pony ride?" Jets turned to Justin.

He hung his head. When his chin lifted, he admitted, "I had no idea Baubles was in trouble. I was chatting up the waitress at Casey's. Once I got here and realized there was a problem, I thought mostly about the welfare of the ponies. I didn't want children to arrive with them in such an agitated state."

"I'll make a note of that," Jets said. "So what else did you notice..."

"Meadow helped me with Sparkles. And she saw Baubles, of course." Justin scratched his head. "Well, maybe the guy they call Thorny. He hangs out on that bench over there. Oh, and Brad May. He sat next to him." Justin tugged on Sparkles's bridle. "But Sparkles here, she's your main witness. You can interview her."

Janis looked over at the wood bench resting against the side of the makeshift barn. Then she turned back to Justin.

"Just so you know, I don't interview ponies over people. I'm a big city cop. I'm not considering some upset equine important because one of you la-de-da animal experts thinks a pony would be a reliable witness." Jets shoved her phone back in her pocket. "So here's what we're going to do.

"Justin, come with me. We'll need to verify your alibi." When he tried to protest, she added. "Someone else can transport the pony parade back to Paws and Pines. I need your statement. Then I'll let ya go.

"And Meadow, you can get on with your day. Go herd those teens." She pointed to Avery and Logan, who sat on a nearby bench. "Put them to work ASAP. I can't have them getting involved in the crime scene like last time."

Janis turned to Sage, a puzzled look on her face. "Is that the same kid as last year? The one we called Elf One? He looks different."

Sage nodded. "Put-on-three-inches-and-grew-some-muscles kind of different. Quite the transformation, don't you think?"

"I'm thinking we need another nickname. Elf One doesn't quite do it. He's a handsome kid. And I think our girl Avery also noticed."

Meadow interrupted. "We'll have none of that on my watch. I'll get right over there and put those two to work. You don't need muscles to wrap packages, and Miss Avery can keep her hands to herself."

6

BECK AND CALL

Meadow McCloud

A sharp whinny cried out. Sparkles rose on her hind legs, pawing at the air. People in the crowd drew a collective breath of horror. One woman held her child next to her body, fear on her face. "We only want to pet the pony," she explained.

"No petting. This one's been through a lot this morning. We're shutting down the holiday ride until further notice." Justin spoke with authority; Sparkles settled her front hooves back in the dirt. He took her bridle in his hand and walked her farther away from the assembled crowd.

"Justin's taking care of Sparkles before he heads to the constabulary," Sage told Meadow. "Why don't you and I settle the elves? I'll go with you."

"Elves are harder than ponies," Meadow stated. "But I'll get them moving."

"They're talking, at least." Sage nodded.

"I see that," Meadow said distractedly. Her mind fluttered, and a realization hit her. *Since discovering Baubles, I haven't thought about the doc's request.* She glanced at Sage.

"As much as I'd like to go settle the elves into their new volunteer position, I promised Doc that I'd look in at Paws and Pines." Meadow glanced at her watch. "I'm already late."

"I can do that for you," Sage offered.

"Thank you, I can manage," Meadow responded hastily. Rather than explain further, Meadow waved at the elves and headed in the opposite direction toward her truck. She didn't want to admit to Sage that the doc was in trouble. Nor did she want to tell her that she'd been assigned to cover up his use of CBD with the dogs.

All of those years, Meadow had sung Doc's praises. And along the way she had deflected Sage's questions about her biological father by talking up the doc. How kind he was. How she was his favorite. How he taught her to ride and work with animals at the shelter. Doc showed up at all the holiday celebrations too. Until Sage finally concluded that he was better than a bio father could have been.

This worked when Sage was younger. But now with her adult daughter edging past thirty, Meadow wondered. Had she somehow taken away Sage's history, making it impossible for her to connect to her biological parents? And had she undermined other aspects of Sage's adult life, like finding her own partner to settle down with and maybe having her own family?

Meadow climbed behind the steering wheel of her truck, still feeling uncomfortable. Mostly with herself. On the drive to Paws and Pines she experienced a wave of anger that made her chest hot. *Not now*, she told herself. *I have so much to do. I don't have the luxury of fanning the flames of my own fury.*

Meadow parked next to the storage shed behind the shelter. She began her search inside. Finding the bottles took little effort. Pet supplies had been stacked in and among the dog beds and clean litter boxes. The people of Lily Rock had always been generous donating to the shelter.

Underneath the piles of beds she found unmarked cardboard boxes. "Better to mix the CBD with the rest of the clutter," the doc had told her a year ago.

"The CBD. Is it just for the dogs?" she'd asked at the time.

"I'm putting together a study on the effect of CBD on canines. If I get a grant, it will mean money for the shelter," he'd explained dismissively.

She realized immediately that she'd made him angry. She'd learned over the years to back down instead of asking any more questions. That was the only way to stop him from blowing up.

But lately she'd questioned her lack of courage. Instead she'd started to take the risk of annoying him further. "Someone said to me the other day that it was so quiet here. That other kennels she'd visited had dogs barking," she told him only the week before.

"What did you tell her?" His eyes narrowed with suspicion.

Heart pumping, she braced herself for one of his full-on temper tantrums.

"Well, what did you tell her?" His voice raised with anger.

"I reassured her that we take good care of our rescues. That's all I could do. At least without mentioning the CBD." She'd been angry with herself after that. Despite her intention to speak up, she'd backed away when it came right down to it.

The truth was that it had taken Meadow years to admit that she no longer held the doc in high esteem. Back then it only took one look at Sage to remind her to keep her mouth shut. She'd rationalize, *The doc gave me the baby I always wanted. He deserves a little loyalty.*

Meadow fumed as she tore open the closest box. Inside the large box was a smaller one. Once opened, it revealed ten bottles of CBD. Meadow knew, since she studied herbs and supplements, that the doc had invested plenty of money. The sheer quantity felt disturbing. *No wonder he's so touchy on the subject. If the inspectors find all of this, they can confiscate it as evidence. It could get quite messy.*

After loading the boxes in her truck, she looked around the shed one more time. *No more hidden boxes,* she concluded. Her search had revealed bins of stuffed dog and cat toys along with the other donations. *And now I'll go to the kennel and then the front desk. I bet there's a bottle or two hanging around reception.*

Meadow removed another five boxes from the kennel. They'd been stored in a cupboard with a leather notebook. She opened the front cover to read.

Dog names with dates and CBD measurements, along with each animal's weight, had been carefully notated. Her fingers tightened around the book when she read the milligram dosage.

She knew that over 15 mg per pound of body weight

was considered dangerous for large dogs; smaller breeds would be half or a third of that. Meadow shuddered.

I'd better check in the back, she told herself. A quick glance into each kennel confirmed her fears. All the dogs were asleep. They didn't look up or make a sound. She opened the cages and checked each one to see if they were breathing. They were deeply asleep but still okay.

With the bottles clinking in her jumper pocket, she hurried out the door and down the hallway toward reception. *One more stop.* Her phone pinged. The text came from the doc.

Done yet?

Meadow didn't text him back. She took a deep breath. Instead of continuing her route to the reception desk, she turned around and went back to the dog kennel. *I want to make certain they are breathing...*

Stepping up to the first enclosure, she stared at a beagle. He seemed to be sleeping peacefully, his small chest moving up and down with each breath. Then the next small dog, an older poodle, was also asleep. He yipped quietly, maybe having a dream. Down one row and up the next, all the dogs appeared to be peaceful. The last one lay without moving. Meadow stepped into the enclosure and then let out a sigh of relief when he looked up before sleepily dropping his head to his paws.

None in distress, she thought. *But they're all asleep. That's not normal.*

Meadow texted Doc back.

All done.

It wasn't until driving home that Meadow realized, *I never did check the drawers in reception.* But instead of returning to finish the job, she put her foot on the accelerator as the truck sped back to her house.

7

THE ARRIVAL OF ELF ONE
MEADOW MCCLOUD

Once Meadow had stored the CBD boxes in the back of her garage beneath a few tarps, she took the winding road back to town. She found Sage and the elves busy setting up two six-foot tables in front of the library window.

"The tablecloths are under my desk inside. I'll be right there once I find parking," she called out the passenger-side window.

It took three trips around the block before someone pulled out and Meadow was able to pull in. She arrived in time to help Logan adjust a tablecloth. "You have to look on all sides to make certain it's even," she explained.

"Got it, thanks." He wore his elf costume from the year before. Green tights covered his legs. Black shorts were pulled over the tights, narrowly covering his body. The pointy black boots made out of felt looked ridiculous. Since it was still warm in Lily Rock, he'd removed the long-sleeved shirt underneath the felt toga, exposing tanned and buff arms. He looked over as Avery arrived with another tablecloth extended in her hands.

She said quietly, "Hey, Meadow. Good to see you. Did I get this one right?" She waved the cloth.

"Yes, dear. It's just perfect. Did you find the wrapping paper?"

Unlike Logan, Avery hadn't changed that much since last year. Her elf skirt rode a little higher and her T-shirt, though snug, wasn't revealing. She'd perched her hat at a jaunty angle and somehow managed to make the whole costume work to her favor. Meadow had to admit that Avery had turned a cheap suit into a fashion statement with little effort.

Meadow also had to admit that together, Elf One and Elf Two made quite a distinguished pair. This year they were both close to the same height, almost six feet tall. She, more willowy, and he of a more solid construction.

Now Sage pushed through the library door. "I found the wrapping paper, at least the rolls. Bows and other stuff are still underneath the counter."

"I'll get them," Logan offered. Once he disappeared behind the door, Meadow spoke to Avery. "So what do you think of Elf One?"

"Everyone's been asking me that today," Avery muttered. "Okay, so I admit, he's hot. Way hotter than last year. Did I forget? Wasn't he downright pudgy and short?"

"I hesitate to say," Meadow commented dryly. "It's not kind to point out people's body types. We're all quite different."

Avery pulled a face. "Come on, Meadow, stop with the bull..."

Meadow's mouth twitched. "We may think those things, dear, but don't say them. Not in front of my library. Nor as a volunteer at the wrapping station."

Avery glared. "Okay, but you know what I mean. You

can talk all you want about not noticing people's body types, but hey. You're old. People my age, that's all they talk about."

"Are you making an ageist statement about me?" Meadow inquired in a soft voice. Her eyebrow was raised, but the smile on her face made Avery laugh.

"Yeah, I am. Sorry. Didn't mean to hurt your feelings. You look pretty fit." She shrugged.

Logan burst through the door, balancing a plastic tub in both hands. "Here we go," he said.

"Speaking of going, I have to run." Sage turned to Meadow. "You're in charge now. See you later."

"Bye, Ms. McCloud," Logan called after her. Then he turned to Avery. "Do you want to make a sign, you know, for the station?"

"I've already done one." Avery reached under her table, pulling up a piece of sturdy poster board, and held it up. It read "Wrap It Up!" in bright red letters.

"That's really clever!" Meadow exclaimed. "I already made fliers that explain our pricing and where the proceeds are going. Before I print it, I'll add the Wrap It Up! part. Then I'll leave them outside along with the tripod for your sign. I think we can open the station now."

"Bork." The tablecloth rose, revealing the shiny nose and furry brown head of a labradoodle.

"Mayor Maguire!" Meadow coaxed him by the collar from underneath the table.

"Bork." His tongue slipped out the side of his mouth.

Logan looked surprised. "I didn't even see him go under there."

"Bork," Mayor Maguire repeated, this time with a tail wag.

Meadow pointed. "Look inside the ribbon container. You'll find homemade dog biscuits. That's what he wants."

She reached over to tug on the mayor's collar. "Don't forget. You're not just a puppy anymore. You're the mayor of Lily Rock. You need to behave yourself. No more begging."

"That's like telling Avery to be nice." Logan smirked.

"Or telling Logan not to be such an ass," Avery said.

"Avery, you are far too smart to use such uneducated language," Meadow reprimanded. "Now you two get to work. I'll be right inside if you need any help."

It wasn't until Meadow stood behind her desk inside that she allowed a chuckle to pass her lips.

8

HIRING BRAD

Meadow McCloud

Meadow unlatched the window near the library reception desk. It was a clear, sunny day in Lily Rock. The air felt crisp and smelled of pine.

She could easily observe the Wrap It Up! station from her place at the computer. An important consideration when she'd agreed to supervise Avery and Logan at the town council.

One glance told her she'd made the right decision. If the elves were busy, then she could keep her eye on the customers. And the cash box. From all appearances the elves seemed to be doing a thriving business.

People lined up along the boardwalk. They chatted while they waited. Michael Bellemare stood in front of the gift wrap table, his arms full of parcels.

"I brought you everything so far," he explained to Logan. "With less than a week before Christmas, I'm glad you're doing this." He put his name on the sign up list with a flourish.

"Hey, Mr. Bellemare." Avery fluttered her eyelashes. Then she looked to the side to see if Logan was watching. Meadow observed her behavior with tight lips.

Unlike the year before, when Logan had followed Avery around like a puppy dog, he no longer seemed interested. He didn't even glance her way. Instead he welcomed the next person in line.

She noticed that Michael was observing both teens with an amused expression, then he glanced inside the library window. Meadow waved for him to join her.

"So you've got our teens under surveillance," he said, standing on the other side of her counter. "Nice work."

"I can see and hear everything," she explained. "At least until it turns cold and snows. Then I'll have to close the window."

"You may make it until Christmas Eve. If we're lucky, by then they'll be finished. Snow is coming according to reports." He looked out the window for confirmation. "But I have to say this wrapping operation works much better than last year."

"Anything was better than last year," Meadow agreed. "When Betty King was, you know, found indisposed."

Michael grunted. "If that's what you want to call it."

Meadow put her hand on the counter, her voice echoing her concern. "And here I thought we'd have a peaceful Christmas this year. But Baubles changed all of that. Will you be helping Officer Jets this time?"

Michael held his hands in front of his body as if to ward off the suggestion. "Not me. I'm no sleuth. I'm not going to be recruited for police business. I had enough of pretending to be her odd-job man just to eavesdrop on her suspects. Janis needs another sidekick."

His smile was rueful. "Plus I've got to get back to Marla's place."

"She doesn't seem to be feeling any better," Meadow said. "I'll be heading over with Skye. Maybe tomorrow. We want to help her winterize the garden."

"She'd appreciate the expert help, I'm sure," Michael said.

"Bork," Mayor Maguire called from outside.

"Seems as if we finally figured out Maguire's true calling." Michael smiled.

"He's been on standby all morning. After a person drops off their parcels, Avery tells them to give the mayor a treat. Then he offers his paw as a thank you. A dog of the people," Meadow said.

"He's better than any politician I know," Michael added.

"Bork!" came Maguire's reply.

"He speaks English," Meadow added.

"Oh, sure he does."

Meadow looked up to find Brad May sauntering toward the Wrap It Up! table. Disheveled in baggie jeans, slung low on his hips, he also wore a yellow Green Day T-shirt. Brad didn't try to hide his interest in Avery as he looked her up and down. "Hey there," he drawled. "How's business?"

Avery batted her eyelashes. Then she glanced at Logan to see if he was noticing. He stared at her, giving a slight shake of his head. She turned back to Brad, this time displaying a wide smile. "Hi, Brad. If you want, you can help us out. Step on over here behind the table right next to me."

Brad needed no further invitation. In a few strides he stood next to her, draping his arm across the back of her chair. He kneeled to whisper in her ear. When she started to giggle, Logan turned away. But not before Meadow saw a look of disappointment cross his face.

"I think we have a problem," Michael commented. He'd been watching too.

"I had no idea Brad was interested in Avery," Meadow said.

Michael chuckled. "He's male, don't forget. She's provocative and pretty. Brad isn't that much older than the elves, for what it's worth."

"Now that you mention it, he graduated from high school just five years ago, but that's a big gap when you're that age."

"It's not Brad's age," Michael said. "I'm worried he's becoming a bad influence. He smokes so much weed. He just seems stuck in his ways. Wandering around town looking for odd jobs. I hope he's not going to lead Avery astray."

"Avery cares about Avery," Meadow said. "She's confided that she's not interested in smoking. I suppose she could do those edible things." Meadow shuddered.

"Just keep your eye out. I'll have a talk with Logan. Poor kid," Michael muttered.

From her view at the window, Meadow watched Michael exit the library and then run across the street through the park.

He's concerned about the youngsters and he's so much better than last year. Michael is a gem. No doubt about that.

Meadow opened the covers of the books ready to be checked in.

"Hey, Ms. McCloud," came Brad's drawl.

In that quick moment his resemblance to his uncle, Doc May, startled her. Same color eyes and the slight smirk.

"Hello, dear," Meadow said.

"So I was wondering..." Brad shifted back and forth, obviously nervous.

"Spit it out, dear." Meadow glared.

"Do you have a job for me? I was helping out with the pony rides, taking tickets. But now the ride is shut down indefinitely. Jets and her investigation. I need something more. To get by." He sounded agitated. But Meadow knew the cause; a combination of anxiety and fear. Brad didn't have an easy life, being on his own without parental support.

"Let me see." She began typing on her computer. "I do have some funds until the end of the year. Not much, of course. But I could pay you minimum wage as a library page. You'd get Christmas and New Year's off."

"How many hours?" Brad sounded more hopeful.

"Just five per day." She closed her screen. "That's all of my budget until the town council approves money for next year. Does that work for you?"

"It has to," Brad admitted.

"But no weed. I don't want any smoking on breaks or dealing in the back alley. Is that understood?"

"Yes, ma'am," he mumbled.

"Good. Why don't you come tomorrow. I'll be prepared to train you. Stay out of trouble until then." Meadow waved her hand in the air as if to make him disappear.

After she closed up at five o'clock, she made her way across the park. Police had cordoned off the crime scene. The tape snapped in the breeze. All the ponies had been taken away.

Only Thorny remained. He sat on his wooden bench, a

paper bag next to him. Meadow assumed it was a bottle. From the way it fit the bag, most likely a fifth of gin. She sighed. As a recovering alcoholic she felt sympathy for Thornton Fletcher. Without his wife, he was adrift. *He may even feel responsible for the trouble she got into.*

And he avoided his loneliness by drinking. Meadow knew that path well. She'd traveled it herself and only recovered with Sage's help and by attending meetings. And now she wanted to help Thorny.

Ducking under the yellow tape, she stopped in front of the bench. "Thornton," she said softly. He opened his eyes.

"Wanna drink?" He held up the bag. When she shook her head, he took a swig.

"I don't drink anymore," Meadow offered. "It's bad for me. It's bad for you too. I can see right now that you're miserable."

"I'm just fine," Thornton slurred. He waved his hand in the air. "Hate all this Christmas crap. Oh, sorry." He looked up at her. "I mean I just plain old hate Christmas. Reminds me of what I don't have. Wish I could just go to sleep and never wake up." He took another drink.

Meadow reached out to grab the sack from his hand. Thornton snatched it away with a scowl. "Leave it!" he growled.

Meadow released her fingers, pulling her hand away. Hoping to placate Thornton, she pointed to his pocket. "What's this?" She saw a metal straw tucked inside.

"Just something," he slurred.

The idea of Thornton carrying a metal straw in the front pocket of his slept-in shirt seemed odd to Meadow. "Do you drink with it?"

"Nah. I just carry it around. It's kind of cool." Thornton lifted it up for Meadow to inspect.

"Yes, very cool," she said softly.

He slid the straw back into his pocket.

Meadow paused to think. The words came in a rush. "You know you can call me any time, if you need help. I'm going to a meeting now. I don't know what I'd do without their support. No one will judge you. You could come along and then come back to my place for dinner. How does that sound?"

Thornton stared at her long and hard. "Sounds great. Maybe some other time." He took the bottle out of the paper bag and raised it in the air. "Empty," he growled, flinging it to the ground where it bounced in the dirt.

"Pick that up," she told him firmly. "It may shatter and hurt an animal."

On her way back to the truck, Meadow felt uneasy. Thornton had had bouts in the past. His binges were well known in Lily Rock. But this one seemed different. Instead of sobering up and getting back to work, he'd just kept drinking. It had been going on for weeks now.

Meadow knew that no one could trust Thornton when he was binging. She knew from her own experience he only cared about where his next drink was coming from. That drink meant more than any relationship, including the one with his own self-respect.

Then as she unlocked her truck, a terrible thought occurred to her. Thorny was at the scene of Baubles's death. Could he have been involved somehow? *Could he be the one who wrapped that rope around the clown's neck?*

She slid behind the wheel. Her mind provided a quick rebuttal. *Not Thorny. Why would he kill Baubles anyway? They weren't friends. Just because he was at the right place...*

Driving toward the main road, Meadow felt distracted. Along with Thorny, she worried about Sparkles, the beloved Christmas pony. How Sparkles was every child's favorite. The prettiest and the one who pranced the highest. The pony who helped Baubles in his act, the one who made children laugh. Sparkles had never tried to nip a child. In fact, she only reared on her back legs when Baubles gave the signal. She wasn't like some ill-behaved ponies.

Not until today. When Sparkles's personality changed. Now she felt unreliable. Edgy. Not herself. She'd witnessed her best friend, Baubles, strangled to death. *No wonder*, Meadow thought. Then she transitioned into another idea.

So if it could happen to a pony, why not a person?

Maybe Thornton's despair over his wife had led to even more alcohol abuse. She'd heard similar stories in her recovery group. It had even happened to her.

Meadow let her thoughts run wild. Maybe Thorny had been drunk. Or maybe—this was the worst thought of all— maybe Baubles tried to get between Thornton and his next drink. Maybe he confronted Thorny, liked she'd tried to do. No telling what Thorny would have done to her, had she actually held on to the bottle.

One thing may have led to another, Meadow speculated. And the rope would have been around the clown's neck before Thorny realized what he'd done.

9

UP TO NO GOOD

SAGE MCCLOUD

Rubbing down a sweaty horse was one of Sage's favorite things. The smell of hay even made her feel at home. Of course she also enjoyed the ride, the different gaits, the feel of the horse. She found balancing her body with the movement of the animal so rewarding.

But it was the grooming that made her really happy. Maybe it was because Doc insisted that she know how to care for a horse first. Before she could ride. He'd shown her how to brush the animal's sides, how to comb the tail and mane, and lift each hoof to clean. How to remove the excess manure from the frog of the hoof. And then how to place the leg down instead of dropping it, just in case it might land on your foot.

Sage praised Sparkles. "Good girl. You've got this."

The pony turned her head, one ear up as if listening. But then she turned back, a shiver running down her body. A soft whinny accompanied the shiver.

"She's very nervous," Justin Young commented from the door. "Skittish from the other day. I'm beginning to think she won't return to the pony circle any time soon. I wonder if she'll ever recover."

He came closer to Sparkles, who stomped her back foot, shifting a pesky fly. "Most don't come back from a turn like that," Justin added.

Sage defended the pony. "Most people would have trouble too. A dead clown right at your feet. Sparkles could have watched the whole thing—Baubles being strangled and all."

"I'm still feeling out of it and I wasn't there for the killing." Justin took the pony's bridle, shifting her head to look directly in her eyes. She took a nervous step backward, avoiding his glance.

Sage heard the sadness in his voice. She asked him, "So how are you with Baubles's death? You're not a pony but you've still got feelings. Finding a friend like that. It's pretty awful."

"He wasn't a friend," Justin added hastily. "We worked together. I didn't know him really. Not even his real name. I'd try to chat him up, but for him it was always about the costumes and 'call me Baubles.'" Justin patted Sparkles's neck. This time she didn't move away.

"But he was a human being even if we weren't that chummy. I've only seen one other dead person. He was in the hospital. Not slumped over by a Shetland."

"I know. The circumstances were so odd. Plus Baubles wore the costume. Come to think about it, I never saw him out of that clown face." Sage walked the curry brush and comb back to the shelf. "I think I'm done here," she announced.

Sparkles stamped a front hoof. Her lips bared, showing strong yellow-white teeth.

"She's just not the same pony," Sage lamented. "She's

gone from the best tempered to mean and edgy in a matter of days. You may be right. As much as I hate to admit it... I wouldn't trust her around kids."

After saying goodbye to Justin and Sparkles, Sage took a slight detour to get closer to the corral when she heard voices.

"No, stop it," came a girl's giggle.

"Come on. Just try one puff. You'll love this blend. I made it myself. Then you won't be so skittish," a low voice coaxed.

"I already told you. I don't smoke," the girl insisted, this time without the giggle.

Two familiar young people sat on a wood rail. Brad waved. "Hey, Sage," he called out.

"Hey yourself," she commented dryly. "What are you two up to?"

"Just hanging out," Avery answered hastily. She'd changed from her elf outfit into tight-fitting jeans and a forest-green sweater. Hair hung loosely down her back in waves; she'd applied eye makeup, her brows darkened, emphasizing her green eyes.

"You smoking something?" Sage shifted her glance to Brad. *It wasn't that long ago I'd be joining them.* Sage stared him in the face, as if he were one of the teens at the academy. She knew being up front was better than beating around the bush.

"Not me." Brad blushed. His hand reached behind his back, and Sage knew he was stubbing out the joint on the wood and slipping it into a back pocket.

"Like I was telling him," Avery retorted, "I don't smoke. Not cigarettes or weed. And I don't vape either. Mimi, my grand, died of lung cancer."

Sage nodded at Avery. "That's a hard way to go. I hope

you two are staying out of trouble." Sage turned to take in a wide view of the property. She pointed to the barn. "The ponies are still spooked, so stay away from the stalls. At least for a while. But if you ever want to ride, I'd be happy to set you up. We have a few rescue horses to exercise. Just say the word."

Over the years Sage had gotten into her share of trouble at Paws and Pines. She'd met a few boys in the barn's loft and if she were being truthful... she'd smoked a few joints in her time.

But she didn't want the teens, one of them her student, to think they could get away with anything on her watch. She considered Avery and Logan her responsibility, even if Logan no longer attended the academy. *As for Brad...*

"Your mom offered me a job. I'm a page at the library," Brad blurted.

"Did she now," Sage mused.

"She told me I'm not allowed to smoke around her." His knee began to nervously bounce up and down on the rail. Glancing to Avery, he waited for a comment. When it didn't come he ducked his head.

Brad just wants to fit in. In some ways he's stuck being a teen. Overanxious for sure.

"See you two later," Sage said. Then she pointed to Brad's back pocket. "Make sure that joint doesn't burn you in the butt."

Walking away, she could hear Avery giggle.

10

THORNY'S DECLINE
SAGE MCCLOUD

The next morning Sage got dressed, braiding her hair quickly and tossing it back over her shoulder. She could hear water running in the kitchen from down the hall.

"Hello, dear. Did you sleep well?" Meadow greeted her.

Sage gave her mom a kiss on the cheek. She poured herself a mug of coffee before asking, "Any holiday flavors?" She held the mug aloft.

Meadow appeared to be studying an old cookbook. She didn't look up. "Freshly ground beans. No flavors," she mumbled.

"At school I make blends, like you do at Christmas." Sage took a sip. "But this is really good, Mom. I didn't mean to complain." *In my defense, what do you talk about after your mom discovers a dead body...dressed like a clown...who works with a pony named Sparkles?*

Looking up from the book, Meadow smiled. "What did you say, dear?"

Sage sat down at the table. *Maybe it's Baubles's death. But maybe not.* Only a week ago, Sage had to ask Meadow when they'd be decorating for Christmas. She'd never been the one to bring up the holiday first. Meadow was always early, shoving Thanksgiving aside like day-old bread, to get to Santa.

"Do you want me to bring out the nativity statues for Christmas Eve?" Sage kept trying to engage her mom.

After two more tries, without any answer, Meadow finally turned away from the cookbook. "I am a bit behind," she commented vaguely. "I'll make you breakfast though."

"That would be nice," Sage replied.

Both women sat at the table with plates full of fluffy pancakes, and Meadow began the conversation. "So have you spoken to Thorny lately? Not just about the weather."

"I saw him at the pony corral yesterday," Sage admitted. "He seems worse than usual. More disheveled. He's never without that paper bag with a bottle inside."

"I am very worried," Meadow said, her voice dropping. "I had a chat with him and I think he may be a witness to, you know, what happened to Baubles. I remembered he was right there on the scene, the first to shout out."

Sage's heart dropped. Though Thorny was a problem, no one in Lily Rock wished him any harm. He'd just fallen off the wagon. That's what they told each other when his name came up in conversation. In the past he'd dry out and be sober for months before it happened again.

"And then he's carrying around this metal straw in his pocket," Meadow continued. "When I asked him about it, he seemed to think it was the best thing ever. As if a metal straw were some kind of prize or something. That seems very off to me."

Now Sage felt puzzled. "I have no idea what a metal

straw could mean to Thorny. Hopefully he's not drinking vodka with it."

"Not that I've seen. But I've heard a lot of unusual stories at my meetings. People's drinking habits that I haven't personally witnessed." Meadow avoided Sage's direct stare.

"Just so you know, I'm sober and attending more meetings over the holidays. And I'm going this morning. Having coffee with my sponsor very soon. She called to set up a time."

Sage felt a rush of gratitude. When Meadow said she'd been to a meeting, that was her way of telling Sage she didn't have to worry. "Thanks, Mom. You don't have to report to me. But I know the holidays and finding a dead body would make anyone jittery. That could shake a person's sobriety."

She stood to clear away the dishes. On her return she brought the coffeepot. As she filled another mug for each of them, she said, "Speaking of Thorny, I'm kind of worried about Brad." By the time she sat back down she'd explained to Meadow about catching Avery with him at the corral.

"Avery made her boundaries clear. I have to give her that. But Brad will keep trying. He doesn't seem to have a purpose, other than wandering around Lily Rock."

"I did find some money to hire him at the library," Meadow said. "I've been noticing the same about him and his interest in Avery. Just so you know, I can keep an eye on him at least until after the holidays."

Meadow really cares about people, Sage knew. *Plus we both have a human project—she has Thorny and now I have Brad. Oh, and the elves. We share them.*

"Is it the time of year?" Sage broke the silence. "I guess the holidays make things more intense."

Meadow admitted, "I've had trouble getting into a festive mood myself. And now with the death and Thorny, plus the concerns about Brad... Well let's just say it isn't helping."

Sage stood from her chair. "Before I go, I have another worry about Brad." She rinsed the mugs in the sink. "I'm wondering if he saw Baubles the morning of his death. He could have been smoking weed in one of the stalls or even dealing. Maybe Brad lost his temper and, you know, strangled the clown..."

"I saw Brad with Thorny that morning," Meadow said. "They lingered while we waited for Officer Jets. I don't know how long Brad was there. He could have been the last to see Baubles alive."

Sage felt discouraged. She'd hoped that Meadow would talk her out of her concerns about Brad and Baubles. But instead she'd affirmed her worry.

Meadow stood up, returning to her cookbook on the counter. "I have to finish this and get to work. I'll keep my eyes on the elves and Brad. I'll let you know if anything suspicious happens."

After Meadow left, Sage tidied up the counters. One glance out the window reminded her again of Meadow's uncharacteristic disinterest in Christmas. Sage only had to look at the redwood fence in the back.

Usually by this time of year, Meadow had decorated it with red bows and swags of lights and greenery. But now a crow sat on top, looking around, as if even he were missing something. "Caw!" He spread his wings to fly away.

Maybe it's time for me to pick up some of this holiday magic for Mom. She's a bit preoccupied, but that doesn't mean I can't do some of this on my own.

An hour later Sage finished the last touches on decorating the fence. She'd even refilled the suet feeders hanging from the oak tree and was rewarded by the flurry of small birds that already clung to the mesh.

Her spirits lifted and her energy returned. *Mom will love this when she gets home.* As she strung the fairy lights, her thoughts returned to the crime scene.

I'm going to talk to Janis and see if I can get any information about Baubles's death. At least more details about the time frame. Then I can talk to Brad and get a straight answer about what he was up to yesterday morning. Maybe I can help remove him as a suspect, assuming he is one.

11

THE PONY WHISPERER

Sage McCloud

Sage sat at Wrap It Up! with Elf One and Elf Two as Mayor Maguire offered his paw. She took it in her hand with a grin. The mayor cast his eye on the container labeled Dog Treats.

"Nice try, you silly mutt. But I refuse to be bribed again." She ran her hand down the mayor's curly fur. "Plus you may have to go on a diet after the new year, just like the rest of us."

"Do you think I can come to your mom's Christmas morning breakfast this year?" Logan asked. "I heard about it from Michael. He says she makes an outrageous cinnamon roll and keeps them coming from sunrise to sunset for the entire day." Logan gave the mayor a cookie, so he dropped his paw.

"Consider yourself invited." Sage looked past Logan. "And you too, Avery." She watched as Elf Two pulled a piece of tape off the dispenser. With expert fingers she turned the package over and folded a corner.

"I'm gonna need more than a cinnamon roll when Wrap It Up! wraps it up. Look at my hands." She held up both, each finger wrapped in a Christmas-themed Band-Aid.

"And here I thought you were trying to be festive," Sage said.

"Paper cuts," Logan added. "Job hazard. I've got them too." He held up his fingers.

Sage slid a bag toward Avery. "I brought this to be wrapped. It's for my mom, so don't let her see." She pointed to the window behind her. "She's got her eye on you both."

"We know," muttered Avery. "Talk about breathing down our necks."

Sage figured that an ounce of prevention was worth, what did her mom say, *a pound of cure*. If the teens knew they were being observed, they wouldn't be surprised when she told them to *straighten up and fly right*.

Sage used this philosophy at work all the time. Being a visible presence. That's why she insisted that the staff eat alongside the students and why she made it a point to be seen during the day. Stopping in on classes, practicing her fiddle, and walking the outdoor paths for exercise. You never knew when a student would stop you with a casual comment that might lead to a mentoring opportunity.

Leaving the elves to their work, Sage walked across Main Street toward the abandoned pony corral. A horse trailer, pulled up near the temporary barn, caught her attention. A sharp whinny came from inside.

Sensing a cry of distress, Sage hurried closer. She stopped at the crime scene tape, her eye on Justin Young, who stood on the trailer ramp. The taut rope he held in his hands made her wince. *He's trying to get a pony to follow him down the ramp*, she thought. *But that way isn't going to work.*

"Come on, Sparkles." Justin leaned back, the rope tightening. Another sharp whinny came from inside the trailer.

Sage slipped underneath the crime scene tap. Not wanting to startle Justin or Sparkles, she spoke in a soft voice. "Looks like you've got a reluctant pony."

With a quick glance her way, Justin nodded. "I know they say people gotta get back on the horse after being thrown. But what about the horse? How do I get her back to her job?"

Sparkles issued a strong cry from inside the trailer.

"Maybe she needs another pony for company. One who didn't feel the weight of a dead clown leaning against her leg," Sage suggested. "A comfort animal."

"Oh, don't think I haven't tried," Justin grumbled. "I took her to the corral this morning to see if she'd hang out with Daisy Mae. Our Sparkles raised her front hoofs and tried to attack Daisy.

"Then I had two problems. Daisy bolting and a bad-tempered Sparkles. I ended up chasing them both around the paddock." He rubbed his sleeve across his forehead.

"Let me have that." Sage reached out for the rope.

"I'm warning you," he said, but then he didn't hesitate to hand over the lead. Justin left her, his boots clomping against the ramp in a quick departure.

Sage released the rope, holding it loosely in her hand. When no sound came from inside the trailer, she inched her way closer. "Hey there, Sparkles. It's me," she used a soft voice.

"Neigh," the pony greeted her. She could hear hoofs scraping against the trailer floor.

Sage took one step closer. And called to the pony again.

"I just want to say hello." When Sparkles didn't object, she took another step, then another. Each time she'd stop and talk to the pony, using a firm but quiet voice.

Inside the trailer, standing next to Sparkles's head, Sage kept talking. She lifted her hand but didn't reach out to touch the pony when she saw Sparkles's eyes grow wide. Sage lowered her hand slowly. Doc had taught her well. To make small moves with an edgy horse, until they begin to trust.

Good ol' Doc, Sage thought. *He is more than a father figure to me. He's a genius with animals. I even apply his teachings with horses to my students when I can. And maybe they'll work with Brad.*

Slow and steady but persistent, until I get the correct result.

12
───────

SIDELINED

Meadow McCloud

"To what do I owe this pleasure," Meadow greeted her friend.

Coiffed and dressed in her peasant-style top, Skye Jones held a book in her hand. "I thought I'd check this out," she said. "Doc thinks I can become more familiar with herbal remedies."

Meadow took the book. "You can always ask me," she offered. Know as the herb woman of Lily Rock, Meadow shared her accumulation of knowledge with anyone who asked.

The fact of the matter was that herbs and remedies were her area of expertise. But now Meadow felt uneasy. When her best friend preferred to read a book instead of asking her, that meant something was amiss.

Realizing it was more than annoyance, more of a trigger, Meadow didn't say what was on her mind. Instead she took a deep breath. Her mother would have told her to count to ten. But Meadow used deep breaths instead.

Then she admitted to herself, *I'm upset because she's assuming she can take over my area of expertise. But what I'm really wondering is whether Doc and Skye are plotting something behind my back?*

After the pause she found Skye staring at her, waiting, with a small smirk on her face. Meadow wanted to shout at Skye, *Mind your own business.* But she didn't. Instead she opened the book, feigning interest in the contents by thumbing through the pages.

"It's to help Marla," Skye explained.

Over a year ago Meadow and Skye were encouraged by Doc to assist their ailing neighbor Marla with her vegetable garden. At the time Meadow was all in.

"Marla is a city girl," Skye had explained to her. "Why don't we show her how to tend a kitchen garden? Just herbs and some flowers at first. I bet she'll enjoy being outdoors."

After that the two friends sat down to map out a design. As the days and months passed, they continued to oversee the garden, encouraging their new friend to sit outside in the shade.

"Take in the sunshine and chat with us," Meadow would say. She even provided a wide-brimmed straw hat for Marla to wear.

"I appreciate you so much," Marla said with a sigh.

And then in the fall Meadow and Skye harvested the herbs. Drying them in bunches on special racks in Meadow's pantry, she put them in vials and containers to make soothing tea remedies.

"I never did ask, but now after all this time," Meadow asked, "what exactly is Marla's diagnosis?" She knew the doc wouldn't tell her, but sometimes she was able to wheedle information out of Skye, who heard everything because she was the doc's nurse and receptionist.

"I really don't know," Skye responded, dismissing Meadow's question. And then when Meadow looked offended, Skye added, "Something about allergies. Maybe autoimmune. He hinted that herbs would be a good place to start treatment."

But now Skye stood in front of her, checking out a book instead of asking a question or two. She'd deliberately bypassed Meadow's knowledge. Not just that, but she made sure that Meadow knew she was being pushed aside by checking out a book in the library. Even though they'd done all the planning together for a year.

Meadow felt replaced. *Know wonder. Triggered*, she concluded.

Lifting the book from the counter, she slid it under the computer scanner. As she handed the book back, she asked, "Have you seen Marla lately? She's supposed to come to my house on Christmas morning. But she hasn't returned my texts or calls."

"Oh, Marla is just fine," Skye said hastily. But not before Meadow noted the slightly brittle sound in her friend's voice.

Skye added, "Doc gave me a list of herbs to recommend to Marla as part of her continuing treatment."

Meadow felt her gut clench. In years past she only needed to hear "Doc says," and she'd jump. But now she felt suspicious. Especially when Skye seemed to be cutting her out of their previously mutual project. Meadow clenched her jaw to keep quiet. But she admitted to herself, *I don't trust Skye with the herbal remedies.*

Meadow knew the power of herbs. Indiscriminately growing, harvesting, and ingesting some plants could cause more harm than good. Over the years she'd been consulted by people who didn't want to be bothered with over-the-counter prescriptions. And then they'd ignore the dosage requirements of supplements since they weren't "real medicine." She'd been able to help some. But not all. On their own, people didn't adhere to the dose and had gotten worse.

Lately people wanted to know about CBD. Those who survived the '60s were especially open to remedies not approved by the FDA. She explained how marijuana and CBD were different, sometimes talking too much. She realized after people acted bored that not every menopausal woman wanted to hear her wax lyrical about the benefits of CBD with hot flashes.

"Why don't you stay for a cup of coffee," Meadow asked. She watched as Skye slipped the book in her tote. "We can catch up." *And mostly I can figure out what you're up to.*

"I don't have a lot of time," her friend explained. "I'm on a break. Doc expects me back in the office."

Once Skye left, Meadow let out a deep sigh. She felt angry and underneath, a little ashamed. She often felt shame when it came to people. It wasn't rational, she knew that, but she also knew it was best to admit the feeling to herself. Her sobriety depended on faultless self-appraisal.

But now, with her nerves on high alert, she began to speculate. And then it hit her in the gut. That feeling of certainly, a definite knowing. *This is about Doc. He's deliberately getting between us, pushing me to the side.*

13

CROSSING THE LINE

Meadow McCloud

Meadow grabbed her purse from under the counter. She stopped outside the library to check in on Wrap It Up!. "How's business today?" she asked Avery.

"Still good. Check out the line." A number of people were waiting.

"Any repeat customers?"

"Several people come by every day. They go shopping and drop off a package. Have lunch and then come back. I bet this is helping out the town's small businesses."

Meadow looked at Avery with new respect. "You're quite the businesswoman. Especially for one so young. Come to the next town council meeting and tell them what you've told me. That way we'll have a clear path for next year."

To Meadow's surprise, Avery flushed. She seemed embarrassed at the compliment. "I'll be going to college really soon," Avery said. "Probably won't come back to Lily Rock after that. But thanks."

Meadow thought as she walked away, *All the young people leave the hill and head for livelier places to live. How can we possibly compete with Los Angeles? Unless you're older and want to escape the crowds and traffic.*

"Bork!" A call from Mayor Maguire interrupted her thoughts. He'd followed her across the street and now stood at her feet.

"I don't have any treats," she explained.

He nudged her hand and then trotted ahead, right toward the pony corral. "Like I said..." Meadow's eyes followed his wagging tail. *He's like one of those tour guides with an umbrella.* She caught sight of Sage, on the other side of the police tape.

The mayor dashed under the tape to greet her daughter. *Janis Jets isn't going to like this.*

"Sage," she called out.

"Hey, Mom." Her daughter grinned.

"You trespassed into Officer Jets's crime scene," Meadow pointed out.

"I did. But for a good cause. Justin is having trouble with Sparkles." Meadow lifted the tape, dropping it behind her back. As soon as she got closer, Sage began to explain in a harried voice. How her morning was spent, coaxing the troubled pony out of the trailer.

"Where is Sparkles?" Meadow wanted to know.

"Over there in the barn. I just finished grooming her. Justin is taking the rest of the ponies back to the Paws and Pines barn. He's got a good heart, trying to bring one pony at a time to reacclimatize them to the scene of the crime."

"I've never heard anything like that," Meadow said with surprise. "I know ponies are skittish. And that particular team has a very good reason." She looked over Sage's shoulder. "May I say hello to Sparkles?"

Sage's eyes narrowed. "You don't even like ponies. What do you really want?"

With a shrug, Meadow admitted, "Just an excuse to see inside the barn." She came closer to her daughter to speak quietly. "I'm wondering if Thorny is spending time there at night. He has his own cabin, but he's often too inebriated to get home."

"We'll have to risk the ire of Janis Jets if we're caught." Sage cocked her head to one side as if in disbelief.

Meadow felt uncomfortable. It was never easy for her to break a rule. She was known to be an upstanding citizen, the town's librarian, with a strict code of conduct.

But now she felt tempted. If for no other reason than Thorny needed her help.

Glancing over each shoulder to make certain no one was watching, she whispered, "Let's get a move on."

Sage giggled. "Okay, it's the two of us on a caper."

Meadow pointed to the barn. "Walk inside quickly; maybe no one will see us."

Sage dragged Meadow by the hand, yanking her inside the tent. She turned to her mother and laughed. "Look at you. I haven't seen you move that fast in a long time."

It was true. Her rapid heartbeat wasn't due to anxiety, it was more a tribute to taking a risk, something she hadn't done in a very long time. Reaching into the pocket of her jumper, Meadow pulled out a tissue to dab the film of perspiration on her forehead. "Let's look around," she said.

"Neigh," Sparkles called from across the tent.

"Do you want to say hi to my mom?" Sage asked the pony.

Sparkles had been tethered in the corner. She stood

amid fresh hay, pawing at the ground with her hoof. But not angrily like before. It was as if Sparkles wanted attention.

"Bork." Mayor Maguire trotted past. He ran across the floor toward Sparkles. The pony dipped her head to let him sniff her face. Maguire's tongue darted out, giving her a quick lick.

"Looks like the mayor's made a new friend," Meadow chuckled.

Having finished his visit, the mayor left, leaving Sage to attend to the pony. Meadow took a moment to glance around the barn's interior.

The Shetland stood at the communal feeding trough that lined one side of the tent. Rings had been installed to hold leads that kept the ponies in check while they ate. Three separate stalls on the opposite side looked empty. Meadow sniffed. Hay, spread over the dirt floor, smelled fresh, making her nose itch.

"Were you here when they constructed this barn?" Meadow asked. She pulled out another tissue to dab at watery eyes.

"Nope, but I heard it went really quick. I mean, it's called a barn, but if you look up you can see it's more like a circus tent. Made of heavy-duty fabric reinforced by PVC."

"So after Christmas, it gets pulled down," Meadow concluded.

"That's right. I thought you knew this stuff." Sage raised a questioning eyebrow.

"Actually it was the doc who brought the idea to the town council. He said he knew a guy who knew a guy, so he's responsible for the decision to hire Baubles. I suppose he'll be in charge of making sure everything is in good order after they're done."

Meadow stopped explaining at the sound of Sage's

phone. "Speak of the devil, it's Doc." Sage held the cell to her ear. "Hi," she said in a bright voice.

Meadow looked away. The doc hadn't called her since the instruction to remove the evidence of CBD at the shelter. She couldn't remember the last time he called her just to chat. She felt as if someone were poking their finger in a fresh wound. After the situation with her best friend in the library, now he was talking to Sage. *Everyone relishes his attention in this town.* The truth was even deeper. She relished the doc's attention and had for years.

As Sage continued to laugh and chat, Meadow's discomfort intensified. She flushed with embarrassment that she felt competitive with her own child. Then she forced herself to admit, *I want him to laugh with me too.* And then an even more alarming question followed.

Is he stealing my daughter and my best friend?

She shook her head, humiliated by her own suspicions. *I'm being ridiculous. Why would Doc do such a thing? I haven't actually told Sage about her illegal adoption. Plus he wouldn't want to undermine our decades-long friendship.*

When Sage ended the conversation, Meadow deliberately dropped her suspicion to ask, "How's the doc?" She made every effort to sound easygoing.

"He's busy and wants to have a late lunch tomorrow," Sage explained.

That's not unusual, Meadow told herself firmly. *Those two have meals together all the time. Wasn't I the one to encourage this connection?*

"Anything special he wants to talk about?" Meadow asked.

"Oh, you know, the usual. He wants an update about the shelter animals, and he likes to hear about the music academy. The students amuse him a lot."

Meadow inhaled quickly. Her jealousy, her suspicions, instantly turned to an icy fear. She looked away to hide her feelings. *I used to think Doc loved Sage, but now I'm paranoid. Maybe he's trying to hurt me through her.*

Meadow wondered, *Does Doc realize I'm pulling away? He's uncannily sensitive to human behavior.* She'd seen over the years how he distanced himself from people who dared to stand up to him, when he'd abruptly turned from former friends, retaliating for selfish reasons.

He could crush anyone in Lily Rock, shun them into submission. And then those people would be isolated and eventually sell out and move away. Her mind, sparked by her imagination, spun like a top, faster and faster.

Maybe the doc has figured out I'm tired of being manipulated. Maybe he knows I'm ready to tell Sage about her adoption. Even though I've not spoken to anyone about my plan, especially not Skye. I'd never tell her. With her decades-long allegiance, she'd tell Doc without a qualm.

Meadow felt slightly dizzy. She inhaled deeply, but her brain wasn't ready to give up. She tried to reassure herself. *Don't forget, the doc has kept us both safe since that first day...*

Something in her expression must have alerted her daughter.

"What's wrong, Mom?"

"It's okay, dear. But sometime after the holidays, I want to sit down with you and have a chat. I've been thinking about something for a long time now, and I want to get it off my chest."

Surprise crossed Sage's face. "And I thought you told me everything," she teased.

"Not quite everything," Meadow admitted. But she saw

the look on Sage's face, the one of longing whenever she spoke about her birth father.

"I used to wonder a lot about Doc, but not so much anymore." Meadow could see that Sage was trying to help by insisting it didn't matter, and she felt Sage's love keenly.

"Let's not worry about Doc now. Like I said—later, after the holidays."

And wasn't that the way. She'd held onto her secret for over thirty years. And every year she wanted to tell Sage, but then every year she held back. Of course, the doc's warnings made her afraid when Sage was small. The threat of taking away her child was too much to bear. Plus she couldn't even prove that she'd adopted her legally.

But after that, once Sage grew strong and into an adult woman, Meadow had found other excuses not to have the conversation. This was when her inner sense of right and wrong conflicted with the lies she'd told over the years to keep them safe.

But maybe this year I'll be different, Meadow thought. *Because Sage deserves the truth.*

14

INVESTIGATING THE CRIME SCENE

Meadow McCloud

"Why don't you check the back stall," Sage suggested.

"Good idea," Meadow agreed.

"I know that one has a cot," Sage pointed to the farthest corner. "Sometimes Baubles would rest during the day. He'd arrive way before sunrise to get ready for his act."

They found a small cot, most likely Army issue, shoved into the corner of the stall. A green wool blanket lay over the top. "Was Justin in the armed services?" Meadow asked.

"Maybe," Sage said. "Honestly, I don't know that much about him. I do know that Baubles was in the Army. A while back he regaled me with stories. How he and his buddies served in Iraq. It's hard to keep a straight face when a clown tells you about carrying a rifle and marching across the desert." Then Sage's expression shifted to sadness. "Hard to believe he's gone. It's like we lost two people, not one. Him being a clown and all."

"Did Baubles get into costume here or somewhere else?"

"He had a room at the back of the animal shelter. Doc was so proud that he'd been able to find him lodging while he was in Lily Rock." A look of amusement came across Sage's face.

"I was working out a horse one morning, and Baubles burst out of his room in full clown regalia including fresh makeup. The guy had a work ethic when it came to his persona."

Meadow felt uncomfortable. Hadn't she been hiding for decades? Not like Baubles, of course. That required an actual costume. But she'd fooled everyone into thinking she was the rule-following librarian, the stalwart Old Rocker, and knowledgeable herbal specialist. All of this just to keep a secret.

Meadow shuddered. More determined than ever to reveal herself more fully, she now looked at Baubles as an example of who she didn't want to be. *After the holidays*, she promised herself. Then she caught Sage staring at her.

She continued her questions about the barn. "Have you ever seen Thorny inside the barn?"

"Now that I think of it, I haven't seen him inside the barn. Just outside on the bench. I don't think Thorny liked ponies that much, so he stayed away." Sage sounded convinced.

Meadow lifted the blanket from the cot. The canvas underneath, water-stained from use, made her shiver. "I can't believe anyone would sleep on this." She dropped the blanket and then smoothed it out.

"I suppose the police went over this place with a fine-tooth comb," Sage said.

"I'm sure they did. But now that we can't find any evidence of Thornton staying here, what about Brad?

You're worried about him. Have you seen him inside the barn?"

"I've seen him go in and out during the day. Once in the morning and again in the afternoon. I suspect he was sharing his stash with Thorny." Sage paused. "And maybe Baubles and Justin. It's hard to know."

"Sharing?"

"Mostly dealing," Sage admitted. "Brad does have expenses. Has to make ends meet somehow."

"Surely he can do better than dealing weed," Meadow muttered. "I have to have another talk with that boy."

"Now that I think about it, Brad does stop to talk to Thorny nearly every day. They sit on that bench and chat. If Thorny's actually doing weed and booze, well that may explain his recent downfall."

Meadow felt alarmed. *Leave it to Sage to put that together.* "I will have a word with Thorny today," she stated firmly. "And why don't you talk to Brad; follow up from your chat yesterday. I did warn him before offering him the library job. He may be tired of hearing from me and welcome a voice from someone closer to his age."

Meadow and Sage looked at each other. "So we've both got men we're worried about," Sage said.

Meadow teared up. *Where did she get all that caring? I'm proud of her.*

Sage's next words came quickly. "Do you think that Thorny or Brad killed Baubles? I can't wrap my head around anyone in Lily Rock being that treacherous. What would be their motive? I mean, Baubles was here part-time. What could he have done that would require killing him before he left?"

Meadow put both hands into her jumper pockets. "Brad and Thorny had opportunity. Maybe Janis picked up some evidence that they were here at the time of the crime. I think both could have strangled a five-foot clown. Even though Thorny is incapacitated at the moment, he's been a construction worker all of his adult life."

"And Brad's pretty fit. And he's young," Sage admitted.

"So that means both Thorny and Brad had means and opportunity," Meadow said.

"And Janis isn't telling us what she's found with forensics. Once she gets all that information she'll arrest someone."

Before Meadow could agree, a sharp *chirp-chirp* came from the road. Meadow flinched. "Is that what I think it is?"

"Sounds like a cop," Sage muttered. "We'd better get out of here before we're caught."

"Is there a back exit?"

"Maguire showed us the way earlier." Sage motioned for Meadow to follow.

15

CAUGHT RED-HANDED

Sage McCloud

As they made a quick exit, a voice called out, "What are you two doing here?" Janis Jets stood in the middle of the side-walk. She scowled at Sage and Meadow.

Sage grappled to find a quick excuse. *If I don't say something now, Meadow will blurt out the truth.* The honest streak in her mother, resulting in a confession to Janis Jets, might make things worse. "We were looking for Thorny," Sage said. "He's not been well and Mom is concerned about him."

That should explain it. Even Janis wouldn't want to pick on my mom for her concern. Everyone knows Thorny is a mess.

"You crossed my crime scene barrier to get in here." Jets sounded dubious. "I don't blame Meadow. She's one of those do-gooders. But you and that Justin Young seem to think a crime scene is a free-for-all. I caught him and detained him at the constabulary."

"You detained Justin? He's only helping the ponies," Sage sputtered. "They need to get reacclimatized to the corral so they can start giving rides again. There's just a few more days and then Christmas will come and go. The ponies will be gone by then."

"And who will do the breaking down exactly?" Jets asked. "According to Justin, Baubles owned the company. Now with him in the morgue, there's no one else responsible. For the ponies or the business.

"We may have a permanent pony ride in the center of town until everything's figured out." Jets sounded perturbed on the best of days. But the situation now had made her even more grumpy. *Then again, she's always like that*, Sage thought.

"Just what I need. A murder investigation and five mammals who eat and poop. And that one with the temper tantrums to boot. This is a nightmare." Jets threw her hands up in the air.

A loud whinny came from inside the tent. "Sparkles is still inside," Sage explained. "She's not happy either. It's your tone and dismissal of the ponies." Sage kept a straight face.

"Is she now. I hope Doc picks up the expenses once you put her into circus pony psychoanalysis. Maybe she needs some self-care time to deal with her trauma."

With her hand on her hip, Janis looked around. "I was hoping to catch a word with Thorny this morning. So did you find him?"

"No," Meadow said right away. "He's not here."

"But he has been crossing my crime tape to sit at his bench every day. You will admit that," Jets added.

Meadow nodded, a grim look on her face. "We've both observed," she said.

"And Brad? I haven't seen him around the barn since the crime," Jets said.

Sage spoke up. "He's working at the library."

Jets drawled. "But I never seem to catch him at work. So typical."

Sage's eyes widened. "Do you think Thorny and Brad are suspects—is that why you've got your eye on them?" *Not that we haven't already thought of that. But Janis likes to be the first.*

Janis drew a blank face. "Could be." When neither Sage nor Meadow said anything more, Janis continued. "I'm thinking that you two are getting in the way of my investigation. Sneaking into the tent, for one. What's going on? Do I have a pair of Nancy Drews on my watch? I can arrest both of you for obstructing justice. Just like that." Jets snapped her fingers.

To Sage's amazement, Meadow, who she was convinced couldn't lie to save her life, avoided answering. Instead she deflected with a change of subject. "There are many stories about amateur sleuths in the library. People love reading the books and solving the crimes along with them. Have you read Agatha Christie? Jane Marple is one of my favorites."

"I don't read about amateur sleuths," Janis exploded. "I have enough trouble as a professional keeping them out of my way. Well-meaning interfering busybodies, that's what I call people just like you two." She pointed at Sage, then Meadow. "Face it, you are both the most well-meaning and busiest of all. Haven't you two got some baking to do? Or other important tasks with Christmas coming up? Leave the investigation to me."

With a sweep of her hand, Janis walked away. This left Sage feeling embarrassed and her mother looking glum.

And then Meadow surprised her by calling out, "Officer Jets. I want to ask you a question."

Jets turned around, an impatient look on her face. "What is it?"

"Did you find any clues in the tent? Blood patterns, perhaps. Or fingerprints. As amateur sleuths, we'd like to know."

16

AT THE CONSTABULARY

Sage McCloud

Jets eyeballed Meadow and Sage. She leaned across her desk. "You two are going to take the ho, ho, ho out of my holidays," she said matter-of-factly.

With great ceremony she marched them across the street. Taking both women firmly by the elbow, she continued the journey past the library and Wrap It Up!. People stopped to stare. Jets's enraged face provided a beacon for all passersby to pause and point.

Everyone in line at Wrap It Up! stopped talking to watch. Even Mayor Maguire lowered his paw, refusing to shake. To Sage's surprise, Meadow didn't duck her head in shame. She actually thrust her shoulders back and raised her face in defiance.

In her office, Jets scowled at them, speaking in a fierce voice. "I can arrest you both. You seem to forget that. Maybe

Christmas Eve in a cell would do you good." She paused to consider. "But there are those cinnamon rolls..."

To Sage's continuing surprise, her mother smiled benignly at Jets. She didn't respond nor defend her holiday baking schedule. Jets's lips turned down. Apparently she'd hoped for something more. At least a bit of resistance from her mother.

Finally Meadow spoke sweetly. "Now that we're here, I think you can tell us a little bit about what you've discovered. After all, we're just acting as concerned Lily Rock citizens."

"Concerned Lily Rock citizens?" Jets repeated in an incredulous voice.

"We do care about Thorny and Brad," Sage reminded her. Then she doubled down in their defense, since Meadow wasn't going to pick up that baton. "From our point of view, they are innocent. Neither one is the type to strangle a clown with his own trick rope. We're trying to make their innocence obvious so that you can arrest the real killer." Sage sat back, clamping her lips shut.

"If only I could agree," muttered Jets. "Come on, you both know Thornton has been spiraling without Robyn at home. And Brad—he's the stereotype for an up-and-coming big-time drug dealer."

"Brad would have to be selling a lot of weed to be considered big-time," Sage broke in. "And maybe we can help him before that happens."

"He may have already crossed the line. I've got a report that says someone is starting up a big crop of marijuana right here in Lily Rock. Once they harvest and start selling, it could attract some heavy hitters. People who want to hide up here in the mountains off the beaten path. Then after the harvest they can take their business to LA."

"And you think Brad's involved in that?" Sage couldn't believe her ears. Brad has stumbled in and out of trouble for years, mostly due to lack of supervision and absentee parents. Plus he had no money to get in on an investment.

Meadow looked thoughtful. "Thornton may be in on growing marijuana. He wouldn't be suspected. His job in construction makes him available to a lot of workers, some who possibly smoke weed."

"I'm not talking the occasional joint here, Meadow." Janis reprimanded. "I'm talking growing and distribution on a level previously unknown to Lily Rock." She sat with her fingers twined behind her head. "And since we're talking, I admit, I found some evidence."

"In the straw," Sage blurted. "It had been freshly laid. I assumed you picked it all up to look for DNA evidence."

"We found blood," Jets said matter-of-factly. "Unfortunately due to Christmas, the reports from the lab have slowed down. But I'm expecting an email any minute now. If you'd just stay out of my business..."

Sage sat up. "You're not arresting us?"

"If I did I'd be in big trouble. The whole town would probably turn against me, making my life miserable." She glared at Meadow. "And by the way, don't you have to start baking? What about the casseroles and everything? You only have a few more days."

Meadow folded her hands in her lap. "You'll be there as usual?" she asked.

Sage felt a surge of love for her mother well in her chest. Meadow's discernment, her voice, and her kindness had turned a difficult circumstance around. Because no matter what happened, dead clowns or men falling off the wagon, Meadow celebrated Christmas with friends. *That's how she rolls.*

. . .

Once Janis bid them goodbye, Meadow and Sage lingered in front of Wrap It Up! to talk about what happened. And then because their seeming arrest was so public, Logan was the first to ask, "Did Officer Jets book ya? We saw the perp walk."

Before Sage could answer, Mayor Maguire jumped to his feet, trotting toward Meadow. He offered his paw to her, and she bent down to take it with a smile. "Thank you, Mayor. I appreciate your support." Standing up, she reached for a dog biscuit and tossed it in an arc into Maguire's waiting mouth.

"We're helping out with the investigation. Janis included us in her inquiry." Sage enjoyed the look of surprise that came across Logan's and Avery's faces. "We had some important information that helped her, actually."

"And that's why you spent so long in there." Brad came through the library exit, catching the end of the conversation.

For once he doesn't look stoned, Sage thought. But the circles under his eyes did make him look tired, as did his wide yawn. To his credit he covered his mouth.

When Brad kneeled to whisper in Avery's ear, Meadow interrupted. "That's enough, dear. It's time for the elves to get back to work."

But Logan wasn't finished with his questions. "Would you like our help? Avery and I can look for clues. I saw you in the tent."

"I have work to do," Meadow replied, brushing him off. She walked into the library.

"Not on your life," Sage answered his question. "You two are wrapping gifts and that's all you need to do for now.

Christmas is in a couple of days. Then we'll need to put all the leftover wrapping stuff back in storage and..." She glanced across the road to the park. "We may need help taking down the barn. It really can't stay here all year round. The Old Rockers will need to come up with a plan."

"Not as exciting as looking for clues," Logan grumbled. "We helped with the investigation last year, remember?"

Avery interrupted, "I have to get back to the dorm after Christmas."

"So soon? Aren't you two coming to our place Christmas morning? Don't forget the all-day cinnamon roll parade and the buffet dinner," Sage said.

A look of surprise crossed Avery's face. "We're not family or anything."

"Meadow and I are family, but we're the only ones. The rest are wonderful friends. Everyone from Lily Rock. So you'll fit right in," Sage added.

Avery tried to hide her surprise, but Sage could tell that she'd touched something in the girl's heart. Avery had been abandoned for the holidays by her parents yet again. *It must be a bit of a shock to get invited by people who are under no obligation to include her.*

As a new customer came to the table, Sage's gaze drifted up to the library window. She saw her mother standing behind the open screen. Meadow's head was bowed and her shoulders slumped.

Sage grew quiet. All the concerns she'd noticed earlier came tumbling back. How Meadow'd seemed out of sorts lately. And how she didn't want to decorate for Christmas. Even Janis mentioned she'd usually be preparing for her brunch by now. Making cookies and freezing casseroles.

Meadow shoved her body back and turned away from the window. "May I help you, dear?" Sage heard her mother speak through the screen. She'd gone back to her dependable self, the moment of sadness covered up, like one of her casserole dishes.

Sage said goodbye to the elves. Then she made her way to her truck. Preoccupied with all that had gone on that morning, she nearly ran headlong into Skye Jones.

"I thought you saw me," Skye said, rubbing her shoulder.

"So sorry," Sage mumbled. "I was preoccupied."

"That's obvious," Skye said with a scowl.

"Heading home for lunch?" Sage made an effort to sound pleasant. Though she'd never been that fond of the woman, Skye was her mother's best friend. In the past she'd explained to Meadow about her feelings.

"Skye's had a difficult time over the years," Meadow said. "You're old enough now to know that she's been in love with the doc since before you were born."

"How can that be?" asked Sage. "The doc doesn't seem to care about her. It's so obvious."

"I know, dear, but the heart wants what the heart wants. And Skye has always waited for Callahan May to wake up and find her ready and available, standing right in front of him. That's why she keeps working as his receptionist, even though he's made it clear that he'd rather date other women."

Sage remembered the conversation and after that, she'd tried to act less impatient. Standing in front of Skye now, she offered another apology. "Really, I'm sorry I ran into you. Would you like to have lunch with me? The least I can do."

"Oh no, that won't be necessary." Skye inched away; she didn't welcome any more conversation. "I have an errand at Paws and Pines. I have to pick up something for the doc. See you later!"

Sage wanted to ask what was so important, but before she could, Skye ducked into her car.

She slid behind the steering wheel with uncomfortable questions. *Mom mentioned that Paws and Pines was going to be inspected by animal authorities. I wonder what's going on over there.*

17

BABY'S FIRST CHRISTMAS

Sage McCloud

By the time Sage got home she put aside her concerns for Skye and the doc. She decided the best thing to do was take action on the decorating situation. *I'm taking charge right now. Once everything is done, I can surprise Mom.*

After parking her truck she rolled up her sleeves, heading to the garage. It only took a few minutes for her to pull down the cardboard boxes stored in the rafters. One by one she dragged and lifted the boxes to the living room.

She started by opening the carton labeled Tree Orna ments. Sage felt a stab of nostalgia. *Mom and I always put up the ornaments together. I wonder if she wants me to wait...* She left that box unopened, shoving it into the corner.

She pulled back the flaps and dove inside another over-sized carton to find two deflated reindeer and a plastic Santa. *Good place to start. I'm going to need a pump.*

By the time she'd returned from another trip to the garage, Mayor Maguire waited for her at the front door. "Hey, doggie," she called to him.

"I brought him over." Logan came from around the corner. "Just looking at the back," he said. "I like the way the fence is decorated." Logan's voice sounded slightly forlorn. Before Sage could ask, he explained, "I was supposed to go with Avery to feed the ponies. I even have carrots." He pulled two from his coat pocket. "But she told me not to come. She's heading over there with Brad and I guess I'm not welcome."

Sage felt for the teen. Though he pretended not to care, she suspected his makeover was intended to get Avery's attention this year. He'd gone out of his way to spend the holidays in Lily Rock again. And now the object of his affection was more interested in Brad.

"You can help me," Sage offered. She shoved open the front door with her hip, the pump in her arms. "Grab that one for me." She nodded toward the box she needed. He walked inside and looked around, eyeing the rest of the stack.

"I like pitching in. My parents never did anything like this. They hired people to put the lights on the outside and put up the tree. Two trees actually. All white plastic. Kinda dumb." As he described his holidays growing up, his eyes stopped at the hearth. "Great fireplace. Wood burning. I like that."

Sage knew instantly that she'd done the right thing inviting Logan to help out. She figured she owed him a story or two about her holidays. "My mom usually has everything done weeks in advance. But she's been kind of preoccupied this year. So I thought I'd surprise her. I assume you can help..."

He nodded eagerly.

Sage handed him the pump. "You can start by inflating the lawn ornaments outside. We can anchor them into the ground once they're up, as soon as I find the stakes."

Logan took the pump from her hand. "Sure." Sage noticed that he looked happier than he had. *Maybe there's something about keeping people busy during the holidays after all.*

By the time Sage hung garlands with fairy lights over all of the doorways and then set up Meadow's nativity set behind the sofa, it had grown dark outside. She checked the time. *Maybe Mom stopped at a meeting,* she thought.

The last thing to do was to set up the tree. Years ago Meadow opted for an artificial one with green boughs, including lights. Sage found the stand first. As she bent over the zippered tree storage bag, she heard a voice from outside.

"I can help with that." Michael Bellemare stuck his head through the open door. "Logan's got everything inflated outside. He told me he was in charge. I found stakes in the garage on a shelf. I hope that's okay. Does Santa look fatter this year or is it my imagination?"

Sage chuckled. "Those decorations are so old, they need to be inflated twice a day due to air leaks. If I work this right, I'll get Logan to come by and pump them up in exchange for cookies. He needs a little distraction from the Avery situation."

Michael closed the door behind him. "Getting colder. Keep the warm air inside." Then he came closer. Yanking the tree from the bag, he stood it up, connecting the three sections. "There you go. Check the lights to see if they still work."

With the plug inserted, Sage and Michael stood back to admire the effect. "It's pretty with only lights," she commented.

"I remember admiring all of your ornaments last year," Michael said. "Let's put a few up just to get started."

Sage hesitated. Her tradition was to put them on the tree with Meadow. But she could hear a note of longing in Michael's voice. It dawned on her that he had no one to share a tree with and that offering to help might be important to him.

"Let's put up a couple and then you can stay for dinner," she offered.

The smile on his face felt like a reward.

The first ornament out of the box was a pony that said Baby's First Christmas on one side, and engraving on the other. "I assume this was yours." Michael held it up for her to see.

"Mom must have known I'd love horses." Sage gently took the decoration from his hand. The colors had faded and one eye was missing from the pony. Sage laughed and handed it back to Michael. "Tell me this doesn't look just like Sparkles."

"It does!" he admitted. Turning the ornament over, he looked at it more carefully. "Do you suppose this was a gift? There's an inscription."

"Let me see," Sage said. She took the ornament back to read the script. "If you want to keep a secret, you must hide it from yourself." She felt perplexed. "That has a slightly ominous tone—for a baby's first Christmas ornament."

Michael nodded. "It certainly is ominous." His brow wrinkled. "And just to make it seem even creepier, I think that's a quote from George Orwell. One of my favorite books, 1984."

The front door let out a squeak. Meadow stepped inside, her eyes wide with surprise. "Are you decorating the tree without me?" She didn't sound pleased. And Sage immediately felt confused.

"Just a couple of ornaments," Sage replied hastily. She knew instantly that she may have made a mistake. Starting the tree without Meadow. And that now was not the time to ask about the inscription.

It was plain to see that Meadow was exhausted. Sage didn't want to upset her, so she reached for an apron that had been tossed over the sofa arm. "Here's your Christmas apron. Time to get baking! Christmas Eve is two days away."

"Maybe later," Meadow mumbled. She shuffled out of the room toward the hallway. "I'm going to take a shower before dinner," she called back.

Once she'd disappeared, Sage looked at Michael. "You've noticed, right? I'm not the only one? Meadow isn't herself this year. She didn't mention seeing Logan or say hi to you. She didn't even take her beloved apron."

Sage folded the apron and placed it on a side table. Michael reached to take the pony ornament that she'd hung precariously on a front tree limb. "Let me hang that one on the back of the tree. It's kinda giving us a bad vibe. And yes, I've noticed that Meadow isn't herself this year."

"You guys ready to have a look at Santa?" Logan spoke from the doorway."Nice tree, by the way. Oh! I need one more stake for a reindeer."

Sage looked around the room. "I can't imagine where it'd be."

"How about I see if I can find one in the garage. We can

always improvise. Why don't you put on that apron and get dinner started. I'm starving," Michael encouraged.

She knew he was only trying to help. Okay, so opening the Christmas decoration boxes didn't go as she'd planned. She'd upset Meadow for sure. And that ornament proved to be emotionally unsettling as well. *Christmas has never felt this confusing before...*

But maybe that was because Meadow did nearly everything for their holiday celebration. Meadow managed their memories too. Only the best ones, like an ornament, could be hung for everyone to see on the boughs on the front of the tree. The rest would be shoved to the back and forgotten.

She tied the apron around her waist and smoothed her hands over the front. Her mom had sewn it years ago. Meadow would wear her apron every year, announcing the beginning of the holiday season. Her mom would make a big deal about the first holiday bake. Dozens of decorated sugar cookies, followed by pies and then the grand finale, her Christmas cinnamon rolls.

Every day in December she and her mom would drop off a baked good to friends in Lily Rock. They'd wear special matching mother-daughter sweaters. And then when Sage learned to drive, she would deliver plates of homemade cookies by herself while Meadow stayed home to keep baking.

After the lighting of the trees in town on Christmas Eve, they'd come back and mix the dough for the rolls, laughing together, singing carols. Sage would take a baking break and play her fiddle while Meadow slid trays of cookies into the oven. "Good King Wenceslas." That was Meadow's favorite.

Sage had to admit that without her mom, she might have grown up experiencing an entirely different Christmas. Meadow was always the one to make everything happen. And now, wearing her apron, Sage didn't feel quite up to the task.

18

LOSING SAGE

Meadow McCloud

The day before Christmas Eve, Meadow lay in bed listening to a crow's caw. With her window open a crack, she always appreciated the sounds from outdoors in the early hour before dawn. But today she felt sad. Not her usual feeling this time of year.

Closing her eyes, she tried to think. *Michael and Sage putting ornaments on the tree. Why would that bother me so much?*

The sight of Sage enjoying Michael's company had startled her for sure. It was as if she didn't matter anymore. She felt left out and alone. Not only were Skye and Doc passing her by, but so was her daughter.

All of those years I've struggled to keep her adoption to myself and now, she's celebrating Christmas with someone else. The habit of rising early and getting to work took over.

As if her body knew what she was supposed to do, even if her feelings did not agree. Meadow took a deep breath and pushed her feet to the floor. *Time to get dressed.*

Once in the kitchen she made a fresh pot of coffee and sat down at the table. Lifting her cell, she texted the doc.

We need to talk.

About what?

His reply was instant.

Meadow paused to consider. There was so much they needed to discuss. The Paws and Pines shelter and his CBD scheme, for one. She didn't want to get more involved with the doc's experiments. And then the secret. She wanted to warn him that she would have to tell Sage. And that she felt terrified that the burden of the lie would undermine her relationship with her daughter. The one and only constant in her life since she moved to Lily Rock.

That's not all, Meadow realized. *I want to talk to the doc about Marla and the herbal treatments.* Like dominoes, her problems with the doc had lined up. Now that she'd begun by texting him, she felt apprehensive. She put the phone down, wishing she'd not sent the message.

Maybe I can slide this time, she rationalized. Instead of telling him she had concerns, she responded with something else entirely.

About Christmas breakfast

Sure, any time.

Meadow slapped the phone back on the table. She

despised herself when she lacked the courage to speak up. She suspected the doc also knew that she was unhappy and that he didn't want to hear her problems, especially if they inconvenienced him. The doc liked women to be seen and not heard. So he didn't mind her lack of initiative. In fact, he encouraged it to keep her in her place.

He's kind of a narcissist, Meadow realized. *Only I've never admitted it to myself. I've been too mesmerized by his power and influence in Lily Rock. And now that I see him more clearly, I'm afraid to question him for fear he will retaliate.*

Standing up to get more coffee, she glanced around her kitchen. The familiar smells of cinnamon and cloves reached her nostrils. She took a few short steps to the walk-in pantry to pull out ingredients for baking.

I'll also need nutmeg and a touch of cardamon, she thought.

Usually the idea of holiday baking made her happy. But not this morning. Her sole motivation was to check the task off a list. Because everyone expected her to make the joy happen. Why wouldn't they? She'd been that woman for longer than she could remember.

"Morning, Mom." Sage planted a quick kiss on her cheek.

Meadow continued to stare out the window. Waiting until the tears passed, she turned to give Sage a practiced smile. "Hello, dear. Good morning. There's coffee."

Then she reached for her apron. Slipping it over her head, she said what she knew Sage wanted to hear. "I have so much to do today. It's time to get started."

· · ·

Meadow slid the spatula under the last sugar cookie. Placing it on the cooling rack, she sighed. Two hours of baking and her mind still felt jumbled. As the cookies cooled she sealed the flour canister, walking the container back to the pantry.

Her mind drifted to Baubles. How he'd been a great imitator in that costume, amusing children for a living. But now that he'd been murdered, Meadow still suspected there was a lot more to him than a few lasso tricks and a nose that beeped.

The more she thought about it—how he tried to be upbeat—she felt convinced that Baubles was hiding something. *Just like me.* Baubles had secrets and maybe that's what had led to his death.

Meadow turned from the sink. This time she texted Janis Jets.

> I think Baubles was hiding something about his past.

> No kidding.

> So you already knew that?

> I had a pretty good idea.

> So tell me.

> Not on your life. Stick to being the librarian and stay out of my way.

For the first time in days, Meadow felt a niggle of excitement. Even though Janis refused to tell her, she knew she could find out for herself. *I'm a trained reference librarian with all the tools necessary to dig in and get information.*

Leaving the cookies on the counter, she picked up her purse and headed out the door. She nearly tripped over Mayor Maguire, who lay on the mat. "You're still here?"

"Bork." He stood up, wagging his tail.

"Well come on. We're late for work. And you have some paws to shake." He trotted behind her as she headed toward her truck.

19

THE RESEARCH LIBRARIAN

Meadow McCloud

Meadow wiped her glasses before sliding them back over the bridge of her nose. She blinked and peered at her computer screen. Since she'd been in such a hurry to hire Baubles the first time, she knew she'd only done a cursory search. But now she took her time researching.

Since the town council paid Baubles in cash, she had no bank records to scrutinize. *Let's see if I can find out more by doing a deeper social media search.*

She smoothed her hands over her jumper. The smell of cinnamon had stuck to her clothing from her early morning bake. But this time she didn't linger over any Christmassy thoughts. She had a job to do. *First his website...*

A person with an orange wig appeared on her screen. The bulbous red nose and the oversized grin stared straight at her. His eyes, obsidian black, looked dull and familiar. *There you are*, she thought to herself.

It took a few clicks for her to discover a social media account. Sure enough, there were photos with Baubles doing lasso tricks alongside Sparkles, his pony. She felt a twinge of sadness watching the duo. Baubles looks so alive on the screen.

She made note of other information, basically where he had performed and some specifics about birthday parties. *I can call those people.* Shutting down the computer, she felt good. Much better than she had in days.

Rolling her mobile cart around the desk, she made her way to shelve books. To her surprise someone was taking a snooze on the overstuffed library sofa. Meadow stopped to straighten the pillows on a pretense, finding Thornton Fletcher stretched out full length. His head on his arm, his face braced against the back of the sofa cushions, he appeared to be asleep. *He must have come past my desk unnoticed. I was so focused on my research.*

She patted his shoulder. The smell of alcohol coming from his clothing nearly overwhelmed her. When he didn't stir, she tried again. "Thorny. Wake up."

He shook off her hand. "Sleeping. Go away."

"You're in the middle of the library," she cautioned him. "You can't sleep here."

Thorny rolled to his back, opening one eye. He lifted his head to look up at her. "It's you," he commented, then lay his head back down.

This time Meadow spoke in her sternest voice. "Thornton Fletcher. You have to sit up."

With a sigh he rubbed his eyes, obeying her command. "All right already. Stop bossing me." His voice sounded thick with sleep. The smell of his breath nearly knocked her over.

Meadow sat down next to him. "Thorny, we need to talk. Your behavior is getting out of hand and I'm worried about you."

"What do ya mean?" He shrugged.

"You know exactly what I mean. It's time to clean up and face the music."

Thornton turned his head away to ignore her. At the same time he tapped at the pocket of his shirt. A worried expression came over his face. He rose to unsteady feet. "Where did it go?" He nudged Meadow's leg with his foot. "You got it, don't ya?"

"I have no idea what you're talking about," Meadow said with a frown.

Bending closer, he ran his hand between the cushions where he'd been sleeping.

"What are you looking for?" Meadow asked.

He lifted up an object, a look of relief on his face. "My straw." He slipped it back into the pocket of his shirt.

That straw certainly seemed important to him, but Meadow had no idea why. "Thorny," she said in a softer voice. "Please come home with me. You can get a shower and clean up. We'll launder your clothes. I'll make you lunch."

A look of hope crossed his face. But he blinked and it was gone. "Doesn't matter. Not hungry." He turned away from her without a backward glance. She watched him leave through the front doors.

Instead of shelving the returned books, Meadow decided she'd better follow Thorny. Hurrying outside, she caught sight of him walking through the park toward the empty pony corral. But before she could cross the busy street, she felt a nudge at her knee.

Mayor Maguire sat next to her. Looking up into her face, he offered his paw.

"Not now, Maguire," she told him.

To her surprise he moved to stand in front of her legs,

blocking her from stepping off the boardwalk. Meadow tried to grab his collar to shove him aside, but he refused to budge.

"He obviously wants your attention." Michael Bellemare smiled.

"Oh hello, dear. I didn't realize you were in town." She pointed to Maguire. "I don't understand why he's acting like this."

"We both know that the mayor has his own reasons for doing things. And I'd say he doesn't want you to cross that street right now. The way he's blocking you...that seems like a *don't go there* kind of message."

Meadow reached to scratch behind Maguire's ears. "I was going to talk some sense into Thorny," she explained.

"We've all been trying." Michael stooped to pet Maguire's back haunch.

"Why would the mayor want to discourage me from helping Thorny out?" Meadow wondered aloud.

"I don't know," Michael said. "I guess it's all in the timing. You can only help people who want to help themselves. I'm not an alcoholic myself, but I do know about depression. I needed to want to feel better first. Like last year. You and Sage were there at just the right time. Maybe Maguire wants you to be patient. At least for now."

"I suppose," Meadow said. "I should know better as a recovering alcoholic. Some people need to hit bottom. But the problem is I don't want to stand by and watch while Thornton risks his health, just to be there when the worst happens."

"I know. A lot of us are watching him. Janis, you, me, Sage, and the rest of his friends on the construction crew."

As they continued to talk, Maguire gave up his stance and walked around Meadow toward the Wrap It Up! table.

He sat next to Logan and offered his paw to the next customer. Meadow looked toward the pony corral just as he finished chomping on a dog cookie.

"Do you want to go with me to find Thorny?" she asked Michael.

"Is it time?" His eyebrow raised.

"The mayor isn't blocking me anymore," she reasoned.

Before Michael could respond, the door to the constabulary flung open. Janis Jets stormed through. She ran past them into the street. Cars honked as she held up her hand, sprinting toward the park.

"Looks like trouble is brewing," Meadow cautioned.

"Let's follow Janis and find out," Michael said.

Meadow took one more glance at the mayor. When he didn't object, she followed Michael.

20

BOTTOMING OUT

Meadow McCloud

"If I hadn't been stopped by the mayor, I'd have been the one," Meadow told Michael. She clutched the handle on the door next to the passenger seat as he pushed his foot on the accelerator. They were following the ambulance ahead.

"You mean the one to have found Thorny?" Michael asked. With a deft turn of the steering wheel, he took the next curve in the road.

"Do you suppose someone deliberately hurt him?" Meadow asked.

"We won't know until they admit him into the hospital and the docs have a look." He reached his hand over to pat her leg. "But I wouldn't worry. Janis called the ambulance before we got there. You were right there on the spot when it happened. In fact it's kind of eerie, the way Maguire intervened and then our conversation about bottoming out.

Maybe this is Thorny's chance, and now we can be there to help."

A slight smile came to the corner of Meadow's mouth. "You can be very encouraging, dear. I do feel better. If I'd intervened minutes sooner, Thorny would have brushed me off. But now he'll be able to get expert care at the hospital."

"Timing is everything," Michael agreed.

"In life and in baking. Speaking of baking!" Meadow voiced her alarm. "I have so much more to do before Christmas. And here I am rushing down the hill with you. Isn't that the way!"

"What way?" Michael braked for the next curve.

"When I have so much to do and then there's an emergency."

Michael's jaw clenched. "I don't think you meant that. As if Thorny were an inconvenience..."

Meadow swallowed hard. She felt her cheeks flush with embarrassment. It was her turn to pat his arm. "Thank you for that, dear. You confronted me and I might even be grateful. No one does that to Meadow McCloud. Everyone assumes I've got things in hand, but the truth is I'm the one who often requires correction."

An hour later they'd parked and were making their way to the Desert Community Hospital entrance. Walking briskly, Michael surprised her. He took her hand and gave it a quick squeeze. Meadow nearly teared up. It had been years since a man had offered her that kind of solace. That quick gesture meant the world to her. She took his arm with both hands and clung for just a moment, right before the glass entrance doors swept open.

. . .

Michael and Meadow stood at the end of Thorny's bed. He'd been bathed and tucked up under pristine sheets. An oxygen mask over his nose and mouth, along with an intravenous needle in his arm, made him seem utterly vulnerable.

But he's not alone, Meadow told herself. *We're here and Sage can visit too.* She'd texted her daughter.

Thorny found unconscious.

Where?

The pony corrals. Janis called the paramedics. Michael drove. We're with him at the hospital.

Desert Community?

Yes.

I'm at Wrap It Up! Want me to close up the library?

Yes!

A doctor bustled into the room. "Friends or family?" he asked them.

"Kind of both," Michael said.

"You're from Lily Rock?" The doctor looked at his clipboard.

"We all are," Meadow answered crisply.

He held Thorny's wrist in his hand to check his pulse,

then made some notes. "Mr. Fletcher came close to dying. Alcohol poisoning. Were you aware of his problem?"

This was the part Meadow hated. How outsiders assume that family and friends control other people, and somehow it's their fault when the person is in trouble. "Our awareness of Thorny's problem is not a solution," she told him tartly. "Thorny is a grown man who drinks too much. That's his to own."

New respect came over the doctor's face. "I didn't mean to imply it was your fault." He pointed to the man in the bed.

"But you did imply," Meadow stated firmly.

She looked at Thorny closely, remembering that it was only a few hours earlier she'd found him on the library sofa. And then how he refused to listen to her, searching for that ridiculous metal straw instead.

"Where are his personal effects?" she asked.

"I don't handle that kind of thing," the doctor replied. "But you can check with the nurse's station down the hall."

Meadow glanced at Michael. "I'm going to do that right now." She left the two men in the room.

"I've got his belongings here." A young nurse held out a gallon-sized plastic bag.

One look told Meadow that the straw wasn't there.

"Is this everything?" she asked.

"Yep. As you can see. A wallet, a stick of gum, and a ticket stub."

"No cell phone?" she said.

"Not that we could tell."

Meadow sighed. "Thank you very much." On the way back to Thorny's room, she realized she was being silly.

Who cared about some metal straw? If he hadn't made such a big deal about it, she wouldn't have thought twice.

When she stepped back into the room, she found Michael sitting by Thorny's bed. His head was bowed and his mouth moving. *Is he praying?* Meadow came alongside and put her hand on his shoulder. Then her cell pinged. It was Sage.

I'm in the lobby.

21

RIGHT RING, WRONG FINGER

Sage McCloud

Earlier that day, before she got the text about Thorny, Sage walked past tables at the brew pub. Instead of finding Doc at his usual spot, she discovered Brad slumped in a chair. He had a beer in front of him. "Hey, Sage," he called to her.

She sat across the table. "Where's Doc?" When he looked disappointed, she added, "Not that having a beer with you isn't great. But he's the one who invited me."

"He got detained. Asked me to meet you and give his apologies."

The waiter came closer. "What do ya want?"

"A large hot chocolate. It's getting colder by the minute," Sage said right away. Eyeing Brad's empty glass, she asked, "You want a chocolate too?"

"Sure." He pushed the empty beer glass to the side.

Sage took a long look at Brad. His eyes were red and he

seemed anxious. It was the way he kept pulling on his baseball cap and fidgeting with a ring.

"Where did you get that?" She pointed to his hand.

"It's something I found," he said. "I asked around but nobody claimed it."

Sage felt her temper rise. "You stole the ring? That's a new low even for you!" She didn't bother to keep the indignation out of her voice. *I have enough trouble with my students. I don't need to be worried about the town's delinquent.*

Brad hid his hand under the table. "I didn't steal it. Don't say that. I found the ring at Paws and Pines."

"Where exactly?" Sage's eyes narrowed.

Before he could answer the waiter arrived, placing two mugs on the table.

Sage felt guilty that she'd been so impatient, especially since Brad seemed contrite. She shoved his mug across the table. "Here, have some of this. You're obviously upset, and I want you to have something other than beer. Okay, tell me everything."

"It started when the doc called me," Brad mumbled. "He wanted me to go to Paws and Pines and grab anything from Baubles's room that looked suspicious."

Sage stirred the whipped cream into her hot chocolate with her spoon. "What do you mean, *suspicious?*"

"You know about animal control dropping in to check on the shelter, right?"

"I heard something about it, but I've been kind of busy," Sage admitted.

"Doc got your mom to pick up the CBD, but he wanted me to look out for weed." Brad took a long sip and then scrunched his face. "Hot," he said before continuing to talk. "And I found Baubles's stash. In a box under his bed. And the ring." He held it up for Sage to have a closer look.

"Stanford." Sage nodded. "Impressive. And here I thought he went to clown college."

Brad rubbed his chin, looking thoughtful. He took off the ring and stared at it. "So there was something else. That I found. In the box."

Sage could hear the anxiety in his voice. *He's bothered by something.*

"Start at the beginning. Tell me all the details," she said, nodding encouragingly. *I can't allow myself to be angry. This may be a very serious situation for Brad. I need to be completely rational.*

"So like I was saying, the doc must have heard about Baubles, how Justin found him at the corral. Because I got a call from him. It was before Janis Jets showed up. So I rushed over.

"The door to his room was open, so I just walked in. I looked in all his drawers and stuff. Man, he had a lot of makeup. And glitter too. Pretty creepy. Anyway once I was done with the drawers, I found this wooden box hidden under his bed. I opened it and found, you know, his stash. And a few papers. And on top of the papers was this ring.

"I knew Baubles was dead, so I just took the whole box." To give him some credit, Brad looked rueful, as if he regretted what he'd done.

"Where is it now?" asked Sage.

"Doc wanted me to put it in the dumpster. But it looked valuable. Kinda cool, actually, with the carvings on the top. So I hid the box. Not at my place, but I filed it in the M section at the library, behind a bunch of old medical books."

Brad looked pleased with himself. "I thought that was pretty smart. You know filing marijuana with the other Ms."

Sage bit her tongue. Sometimes Brad exasperated her, and this was one of those times. He seemed so childish. "Well I want you to give me that box. We're going to walk over to the library right now. I just hope no one else has noticed it."

"I can drive." He looked skeptical.

"No, you can't." She pointed to his empty beer glass. "Plus the walk will do us both good." Sage glanced at her phone. "If we hurry we can make it before the library closes."

22

IN THE STACKS

Sage McCloud

By the time Sage and Brad arrived, three people stood in line at Wrap It Up! Avery stuffed a wad of red tissue into a decorative bag. "That should do it." She handed the bag to a mom with a baby in her arms.

"Perfect." The woman moved aside, making room from the next customer.

"Do they even know what they're wrapping?" Brad whispered in Sage's ear.

"It's looking pretty regimented now," she admitted. "They're on autopilot. Maybe the thrill is gone." Sage glared at Brad. "You can talk to your girlfriend later. Let's find what we came for."

She held the door for him. Once inside they made their way across the library.

"It's over there." He pointed to the stacks. "Like I said, in the..."

"M section. Got it." Sage walked ahead of Brad. She ran her finger along the volumes, stopping in front of an impressive array of medical reference books.

Brad removed two and handed them to Sage.

"Still there," he told her in a hoarse whisper. Sliding the box out to the edge of the shelf, he held it and then tucked it under his arm. Then he took the two volumes from Sage and put them back on the shelf.

She removed the box from under his arm. Staring at the design carved into the wood, she lifted the lid. She found a plastic bag with marijuana leaves and a few rolling papers tucked underneath. She held out her open palm. "Hand over the ring. I'm going to replace it and then we're going next door to talk to Janis."

When his face registered disbelief, she added, "Yep, you're coming with me.

"I won't tell her that you wore the ring if you don't. We can keep that little secret between ourselves."

With a sheepish grin, Brad slid the ring off his finger. "It was dumb to take it. I know that now. Sometimes I'm kind of..."

"Impulsive," she said. "And that's what we're going to talk about right after Christmas. How you need to grow up and find other employment that doesn't include being the weed dealer of Lily Rock. That impulsiveness will get you into deeper trouble if you're not careful."

He hung his head. "I know. You're right."

Sage let her words sink in, especially the warning tone she'd perfected since working at the academy. Then she asked, "Did you tell anyone else where you hid that box? Avery, for instance?"

Brad blushed. He stammered, "Maybe, kind of... I mean, we were sitting around the shelter with Justin the other day.

I may have mentioned that I found the box in Baubles's room and got ahead of the cops. I was trying to impress her."

Sage wanted to shake Brad until his teeth rattled. Not only had he gotten himself in trouble, but he may have dragged Avery in with him. Swallowing back her retort, she counted to ten.

She realized that Brad wanted to be better but that he'd easily misplace his resolve when something or someone captured his attention. Spending his time at Paws and Pines wasn't helping.

She had to admit the atmosphere there had changed over the years. When she was younger, the shelter was the perfect place for her to hang out. Meadow knew she was safe with the animals and with Doc's supervision. But now the shelter felt sketchy. Maybe Doc wasn't as concerned. Sage couldn't put her finger on the cause. But she knew that Brad contributed to the atmosphere and that he'd used the shelter for alone time with Avery.

But if I come on too strong, he'll hide his problems from me. And that might be worse. "Come on. Let's have that chat with Janis." She tapped him on the shoulder. "I want you to tell her just what you told me."

"That the doc called and told me to look in Baubles's room?" He appeared surprised.

"Yep, that first. And then what you found. Just so you know, I'm concerned that the doc involved you. Maybe he's not thinking right. He's most likely nervous about the inspection. I don't know. But I do know that you don't need to be encouraged to go sneaking around people's rooms. You get into enough trouble with your own bad ideas."

23

FALSE BOTTOM

Sage McCloud

Brad and Sage sat across the desk from a scowling Janis Jets. She held the carved wooden box in front of her. With latex gloves covering both of her hands, she opened the lid and then let out a big sigh. Lifting each item one by one—first the baggie with weed, then the ring, and finally the rolling papers—she set them all aside.

To Sage's surprise, Janis turned the box over. She tapped it with her fingers. Then she bumped the box against the side of her desk. She looked inside again. Her voice sounded nostalgic. "I used to have a box like this when I was a kid. I'd hide stuff underneath in the false bottom so my mom wouldn't find out. Mom was such a snoop."

Jets used a letter opener to poke at the snug-fitting felt bottom. Easing it away, she lifted by the corner. "Just as I thought," she announced.

Janis lifted a small stack of cards, small enough to fit in the palm of her hand.

"I used to be critical of Mom," Janis continued. "But then I realized that I'm a snoop too. I've made a living of poking into other people's lives. In some ways Mom was my mentor."

She held up the papers with a big grin. "Only I put my super detective power to good use. Mom just butted into my business."

"What are those?" Brad leaned over the desk to have a closer look.

"Messages, I think. Ones that Baubles didn't want anyone else to see," Jets said.

"Probably prompts for his secret magic tricks," Sage suggested. Holding the first note up, Janis's eyes narrowed.

"If you look, you'll see this ain't magic." She waved the note at Sage. "We've got small cut-out letters, glued on." She spread four cards on the desk, reading each one aloud. "I know who you are." Janis shoved it aside. "You can't hide," Jets read. "Watch your step." She put that one down with the others.

She inhaled and read the last card. "Ready to die?" Jets turned the card around for Brad and Sage to see for themselves. When Brad reached to pick up a note, she slapped his hand.

"You can't touch those, dummy. Just what I need, your fingerprints."

Sage felt her nose tickle. She sniffed. *Does Janis have Christmas cookies in her desk?* "What's that I'm smelling?"

Jets ran her finger over the inside of the box. She lifted her hand. A brown residue covered the tip. "There's dust." She held the box under her nose. "That's odd. Smells like cinnamon."

"Really?" Sage said, puzzled. "Maybe to disguise the weed smell? Baubles wasn't a baker or anything."

Jets held one of the notes in the air. From across the desk, Sage could see a brown film covering the back of the paper. "It's all over this one." Janis inspected the rest. "And these too. Why would that be? Is it deliberate and is it from Baubles or the person who sent the threatening notes..."

Jets sat back in her chair, shaking her head. "I'll get these to the lab. Maybe they will get more answers. It seems someone planned on killing Baubles. They sent these cards as a warning."

"But why didn't Baubles bring these to you? Ask for protection?" asked Sage.

"I don't know. But like I said, to the lab they go. Now for this..." Janis picked up the ring from her desk. "Do you suppose he graduated from Stanford? I find that hard to believe. A guy that smart playing with a pony and doing rope tricks for a living. What a waste of tuition. His parents must have been very angry."

Brad looked away. He fidgeted in his chair.

Jets put the ring down and looked at him with a steely expression. "So you stole this box out of Baubles's room right after he died? That's pretty suspicious. If I didn't know better, I'd think you were up to something."

"Doc told me to do it," he muttered.

Jets looked thoughtful. "So you work exclusively for Doc now, at Paws and Pines?"

"Kind of," Brad said. "Except for the next week or so. Meadow offered me part-time at the library."

"Good for her. But I want to know what you do for the doc."

"I help out in reception. And I take care of the dogs, you know, feed them and clean up poop."

"You know there's going to be a big inspection about Doc's use of CBD," Jets said.

"He told me." Brad's voice sounded clipped. "Can I go now?" He glanced longingly toward the door.

"Not before I issue an official warning. Stay away from anything to do with this investigation." Jets's voice sounded firm. "That includes Baubles's room. The pony corral and tent. And Sparkles too. I've been checking in on her and she'd probably enjoy giving you a good kick if you're not careful."

"Yes, ma'am," he said quietly.

"If you don't stay away," Janis's smile widened as she warmed to her lecture, "then I'll have to put you in a cell. And I don't care if it's Christmas either. So keep your nose away from the shelter and out of my police business. Got it?"

"Yes, ma'am," Brad repeated, his voice very low.

Sage followed Brad out the door. "That could have gone a lot worse," she told him.

"I suppose," he replied.

Crisis averted. Janis does have a heart. She must have realized that Brad meant no harm.

24

SOBERING UP

Meadow McCloud

Meadow's eyes drifted toward the hospital bed. Closing her book, she removed her reading glasses. Thorny lay with his hands folded on his chest, eyes closed. The doctor assured her it was only a matter of time before he'd regain consciousness. And finally, Thorny did just that. His eyes opened slowly, more like Sleeping Beauty, a slight smile on his lips.

"Hello, dear," she said softly.

His eyes shut as quickly as they opened.

Meadow knew he dreaded a conversation with her. Sleeping Beauty got a kiss from a handsome prince, but Thornton was most likely anticipating a lecture on sobriety.

Familiar with the signs of alcohol poisoning, Meadow knew how close he'd come to dying. She also knew that when he woke up, he'd appreciate seeing her at his bedside once the lecture was over. But before she could urge

Thornton to open his eyes again, she heard a voice from the doorway.

"Hey, Mom." Sage stood inside the room. "It took a minute for me to get permission to come up. I had to say I was Thorny's daughter." She smiled sheepishly.

Meadow took her by the hand. "Thank you for coming." She nodded to Thorny. "Pull up another chair. I can fill you in on the doctor's report."

After Meadow had finished telling Sage all the news about Thorny, she felt relieved. "I feel so sorry for him. Maybe this will scare him enough that he'll want some help." Meadow knew full well that there was a good chance Thornton could hear every word. This was her way of telling him without being in his face. She hoped it would work.

A low sound came from Thorny, as if he were trying to clear his throat.

Meadow stood from the chair and leaned over the bed. "Thornton, dear. Are you awake?"

"Yeah," came his reply. "Why are you talking?"

"Sage and I are right here, dear."

One eye fluttered and opened. He looked past Meadow to Sage.

"I have a terrible headache," he said.

"Dehydration," Sage responded immediately.

Meadow flinched, feeling the familiar guilt that spread over her chest, smothering her sense of well-being. Not because Sage wasn't right, but because her daughter was so familiar with the symptoms of alcohol poisoning. And she'd been the one to teach her. Meadow adjusted her voice to sound encouraging.

"That's right, Thorny. The IV will plump you right up.

Once you're hydrated the headache will improve." When he didn't respond, she added grimly, "I should know."

Meadow sat back down in her chair holding his hand firmly in her grasp.

As Thorny coughed and sniffled, Meadow waited. Once there was a pause, she asked, "Do you remember how you got here?"

"Not really." He closed his eyes again.

"Do you remember me finding you asleep in the library?"

"Nope," he said.

"Or when the paramedics picked you up at the pony corral?"

His eyes fluttered open. "I don't remember any of it, Meadow. Blacked out. Gawd, I feel just terrible." A tear rolled down his cheek.

Meadow's resolve doubled at the sign of his remorse. In the past she'd back off and comfort him, but today... *He nearly died, and if something doesn't change, he'll do it again.*

"Stop feeling sorry for yourself right now." She used a steady and firm voice. "It's time for you to take charge of your life. What would Robyn say if I told her? She'd be so disappointed in you, going all to pieces."

Thornton squeezed his eyes tighter, reminding Meadow of a small boy.

"Not looking at me isn't going to stop me from telling you the truth, Thornton Fletcher. If anything, you're in more trouble now. With Sage as my witness, once you leave here you're coming home with us."

Sage's eyes widened. But Meadow knew her daughter recognized an intervention when she saw one, and she confirmed that by keeping her mouth closed.

Thorny finally spoke. "Oh all right. I'll come home with you if I have to. I wish Robyn were here." He turned on his side to face the wall.

Sage whispered to Meadow. "Tomorrow is Christmas Eve. Are you sure you want a houseguest?"

Meadow's bottom lip trembled. "Someone has to take him in hand. Might as well be me."

Then she stood and leaned over the bed, saying in a firm voice, "Don't go to sleep again. I have another question." Thorny rolled on his back. He opened his eyes, blinking to focus. This time the tears were gone.

"What's that?" he asked.

"The metal straw. Do you remember where you put it?"

"What metal straw?" His brow wrinkled.

"The one you've been carrying in your pocket the past few days." Meadow pointed to his chest where the pocket would have been, had he not been wearing a hospital gown. "You were very concerned about it in the library. And then when I went through your personal effects, it was missing."

"For the life of me," Thornton wailed, "I can't remember a metal straw. For that matter, why would I want one? I don't use those things. They're for children, not grown men." Thornton rolled his eyes.

Meadow sat back down. She wasn't sure why that straw seemed so important. Maybe it was because Thorny had been so adamant about keeping it close. But now he didn't remember.

His voice floated from the bed. He sounded very tired. "Maybe it belonged to that dead clown. The straw. I have a vague recollection I found it near the body. But then..." A snore came from the back of his throat, blocking out any more words.

25

CHRISTMAS EVE MORNING

Meadow McCloud

Meadow dressed quickly and made her way to the kitchen. She found Sage already leaning over the counter next to the coffee maker. One glance past her daughter's shoulder through the window toward the back fence brought a gasp of surprise. "I just noticed. You decorated out back."

"I did." Sage handed her a brimming Christmas mug, covered with dancing snowmen. "All by myself. Oh, and there's your apron." She pointed to a hook.

"It's Christmas Eve morning," Meadow said. "I haven't started my baking, I should've woken up earlier."

"I can help," Sage offered. "You have been a bit preoccupied with Thornton."

"The doctor left me a message last night. Thornton will be discharged today before lunch." Meadow reached for her cell phone and nervously thumbed through her messages before clicking the phone off.

She pulled out a kitchen chair. "Have a seat. You seem stressed."

Meadow sat down, feeling her lower back stiffen. "I haven't done my usual stretches for ages."

"The holidays throw so much at us." Sage sat in the chair to face her mother. "But tomorrow is Christmas, so we'd better get on this. How many people did you invite to drop in and stay for dinner?"

When Meadow was finished reciting the list, Sage added, "And don't forget Thornton, Logan, and Avery. I included them."

"Two elves for Christmas. I'm glad they can come." Meadow smiled.

Sage took a sip of coffee. "I know this isn't your usual tradition," she began, her voice sounding hesitant.

Meadow braced herself. Any sentence like that from Sage only meant she wasn't going to like it, at least at first. "What do you mean?"

Sage patted her mother's hand. "I'm thinking of letting the elves stay overnight for Christmas Eve. They'll be right here the next morning to join in and set out the plates and cutlery, that kind of thing. And I know Logan would like to help with the baking."

"Logan would do anything to be around Avery," Meadow said.

"That too. So let's put them to work. Bring them into our Lily Rock tradition. It's for a good cause. Plus you're busy saving Thorny and I've had so many issues with Brad. I didn't get to tell you the latest. Brad let himself into Baubles's room right after he died. And Janis was so mad!" Sage explained the interview with Jets the day before. And all about the threatening notes.

Meadow bristled. "That's just dreadful! Imagine having

to threaten a clown like Baubles. All he ever did was make people laugh. Remember how he'd lasso a child and tug them along and then put them on Sparkles's back for a ride?"

"And what do you think about the cinnamon?" Sage asked.

"I can't even imagine why cinnamon would be relevant to a murder investigation. Maybe someone used the box earlier to store herbs or... I know! Maybe the cinnamon was to cover up the smell of the pot. It is a powerful spice."

"I thought the same thing " Sage admitted. "And that's not all. Sparkles isn't getting better. Oh she has her calm moments, but then she reverts back and is all nervous. I don't know if she'll ever get back in the pony ring again."

"It would be a shame if that's the case." Meadow paused to think about the pony. "Maybe Sparkles feels as if everything changed." She felt her eyes grow moist. "Baubles's death took away Sparkles's life purpose and the person she loved best. That's a double blow."

Meadow had to admit to herself that she identified with the Shetland pony. Wasn't that what she was afraid of if she told Sage the truth? That her life purpose of being a mother would no longer be relevant and that Sage might turn her back and leave because once she knew the truth, she'd feel betrayed.

Meadow swallowed her last sip of coffee. *Should I tell her now?* She looked at her daughter, who was making a list of things to do before Christmas day. *Why derail her now? She's so busy and quite happy too. I can't. Not at Christmas. Maybe after the holidays. I'll broach the subject then.*

26

THE PHONE CALL

Meadow McCloud

Later that morning Meadow called the hospital and connected with Thornton's nurse. "He'll be ready by one o'clock," she said brightly. "Have to get everyone discharged before the annual Christmas Party."

Meadow hung up a little disgruntled. *Don't they care about patients over parties?* But then she realized she was in a similar situation. Rushing about getting everything ready instead of really paying attention to people's feelings.

Everyone expected her Christmas open house to happen just as it always had, year after year. The words "but you've always done it that way" echoed in her mind.

Thornton's health crisis. The death of Baubles. Brad's potential impulsiveness. Even her own sobriety didn't matter. The party must go on!

Pushing aside the unspoken expectations, Meadow prioritized, knowing she had another important phone call to make. She knew that call might be the way forward for Thornton and his road to sobriety.

After the initial greeting, the warden assured her, "We can arrange that. Mrs. Fletcher has been a model inmate. By the way, we're ready to recommend her for early parole."

"That's very good to hear," Meadow said. "Her husband will be at my house for the holidays and..."

She felt much happier with herself after the call. Even if Thorny didn't like staying with her, he'd appreciate what she'd done. And he'd most likely welcome Michael's company on Christmas day.

She'd tested her theory with Michael just to make certain. One request and he'd happily agreed to pick up Thorny after his discharge. "Sure, I'll bring him to your house." Michael sounded quite chipper. "You know I like keeping busy at Christmas. Anything else I can do?"

She assured him that was quite enough.

Meadow picked up her flour canister first. It took her a few trips back and forth from the pantry to arrange all of her baking ingredients next to the flour. The last thing to transport was her oversized red bread bowl.

It had a chip on the edge, but that didn't matter to Meadow. She continued to use it year after year for sentimental reasons. It was a gift from her mother before she passed away. And Sage realized, even as a small child, that the red bowl came out the Friday after Thanksgiving; the bowl was a symbol of all things Christmas. *Better late than never*, Meadow consoled herself crossly.

Then she remembered Sage's idea about the elves. *I suppose it will work. This afternoon I'll help the elves with the last-minute wrapping. We can put everything away in the library and after they change clothes, they can come back home with me.*

Later than usual, she headed to her truck to get to the library to open the doors. Mayor Maguire waited for her in the driveway. "Stay right there," Meadow told him and ran back toward the house.

She returned quickly, this time holding a Santa hat. Placing it on Maguire's head, she slipped an elastic tie under his neck, securing it in his scruff of fur. "A merry ho, ho, ho to you." She adjusted the hat so that the white bobble wouldn't poke him in the eye.

Driving into town, people pointed at Maguire in the passenger seat. Children, their noses pressed to car windows, laughed at the dog. Meadow, hands on the wheel, glanced over to check on Maguire. He seemed to be taking his role of Santa dog seriously, sitting up in the seat, his mouth hanging open in a smile. But Meadow felt the chilly air; instead of closing his window, she turned on the heat.

The line in front of Wrap It Up! wound past the constabulary and around the corner. People dressed in coats and gloves wrestled with shopping bags. Meadow stood with her hands on her hips. "We'd better have a cut-off time or you'll be here all night," she told the elves.

"Can't stop," gasped Avery. "Look at all of these." She pointed to the baskets filled with unwrapped gifts. "We have to get them done."

"But I want to start baking." Logan slapped a bow on a box. "We're still going to help at your house, right?"

"Yes, dear. I've set all the ingredients on the counter already. Don't worry, I won't start without you."

"How about I make another sign?" Avery interrupted. She lifted the Wrap It Up! poster board and scribbled on the back. "This way we'll have a more definite closing time." She'd printed *Five O'Clock Closing* in big bold letters. Meadow nodded.

"I'll leave you to it then." She turned away from the elves and walked through the library entrance.

Behind the counter Meadow clicked on her computer. She shivered. "Brr." She pulled her jacket around her to keep warm. "Maybe we'll get snow on Christmas this year."

After inputing the book returns, she rolled her cart toward the stacks and then stopped with a gasp. *What's gone on here?* Books had been strewn onto the floor. She left the cart to examine the disarray.

Medical resource volumes had been left in a heap. Others on the top shelf lay on their sides. Frustrated, she stamped her foot. "We'll just see about that!" Pushing her cart out of the way, she hurried toward the resource counter. After bringing up the CCTV view, she found footage from the past twenty-four hours.

Sure enough, someone dressed in jeans and sneakers frantically searched behind the books in section M. A blue hoodie pulled around their head made identification impossible. Though she couldn't see the face, the body looked tall and thin. Meadow watched the video again. *That could be any one of a number of people*, she thought.

Meadow made the image bigger and watched again. Unfortunately she couldn't tell if the person was male or female. Feeling discouraged, she shut down the view right as the computer dinged an email alert.

A new message flashed on her screen.

Clicking to open the email, she saw that the message had been sent by Jim Abernathy. He'd left his phone number so that she could call him.

Cell in hand, she tapped his number and waited.

"This is Jim," came a man's voice.

"Yes, I'm Meadow McCloud. The research librarian in Lily Rock. You left a message with your number." She continued to explain, "Like I mentioned in my email, I noticed that you hired Baubles the clown for a recent family birthday party. Do you happen to have his contact information and his given name? I'd like to get in touch."

"I do," the man's voice dropped off at the end. He sighed.

Meadow could tell that the man on the other end of the phone was not going to give her a quick answer. He inhaled deeply and began.

"My whole purpose in planning that party was to make another attempt at getting in touch with Bobby. He showed up, but it didn't stick. After the cake and ice cream he took the check and we didn't hear from him again.

"He refused to pick up the phone when I called. So in answer to your question...Bob Abernathy is Baubles the Clown. Family called him Bobby. Here's his personal cell number."

Meadow pulled a paper out of her drawer. She made a note. "And you are his brother?"

"That's right, he's my baby brother," the man stated flatly.

Meadow felt her heart beat faster. *Do I tell him? Christmas Eve, the worst time to break bad news.*

She cleared her throat. "Mr. Abernathy. I'm afraid I have some bad news."

"Not again," he stopped her from continuing. "I don't mind giving you his number, but I'm done. I've spent years trying to make things right with him. If you're trying to get us back together, you wouldn't be the first. I can't do this anymore."

Before Meadow could speak again, the phone clicked and they were disconnected.

I guess I'm not the only one who runs away from bad news this time of year.

27

THE SLEEPOVER

Sage McCloud

Sage watched Logan tie the bow on his last package. "Do you want help closing up shop?"

"That would be great." He slapped a gift tag on a box and handed it to a woman. "Here you go," Logan said.

The woman took the parcel and turned to Mayor Maguire. "Happy Christmas, Mayor." She patted his head and offered a treat.

"We have one more present. No one picked it up!" Avery held a flat box in the air. "It says it's supposed to go to Janis Jets."

"That's the only gift that's required an actual recipient on the tag. I don't know who dropped it off," Logan said. "But I guess we can take it to her. She's right next door." He walked away humming "Jingle Bells" under his breath.

While Logan made the delivery, Sage helped put away the leftover ribbons and boxes in the storage container, then topped them with the remaining sheets of wrapping paper. Avery folded the tablecloths and laid them on top. Logan returned in time to collapse the tables.

Turning to Sage, he asked, "Can we leave all this stuff behind the library reception counter until after Christmas?"

"Of course." Sage knew her mother was used to picking up the remnants of the holiday. Sometimes it took her weeks to get everything returned to storage.

Once they'd put the storage containers inside, Sage warned, "We have to get home pretty quick to work on the baking. Before the tree lighting."

"I just want to get out of this elf outfit," Avery moaned. She removed her hat and shivered, looking toward the darkened sky. "Do you think it will snow?"

"That would be fantastic," Logan interjected. "I think snow on Christmas is the perfect decoration, don't you?"

Avery rolled her eyes. "The perfect Christmas would mean neither of us had to stay at the dorm. We'd be skiing or having a drink by the fire at some resort. Maybe opening gifts. Expensive ones. With a family who cared."

Sage felt her heart drop. *They've been doing so much for others this week. I hope they're not disappointed with Christmas.* "The tree lighting is beautiful," she commented. "And Mom's cinnamon rolls can't be beat. Come on, you two."

Avery pulled her coat closer to her body as Sage kept talking, trying to cheer them up. "The smell of baking in the morning, especially on Christmas... There's nothing I like better. Why don't you two stay at our house tonight? We have extra sleeping bags and you can curl up by the fire."

"On the floor?" Avery sounded shocked.

Logan, his voice overly chipper, piped in. "Maybe we can dig up a couple of air mattresses."

"No need to dig," Sage said. "We've got two in the garage."

"Bork," called Mayor Maguire. Brakes screeched as a red BMW came to a sudden stop. He made his way across the street toward them, the pom-pom on his hat bouncing in the air.

"Hey, Mayor." Logan bent to scratch his neck. He turned to Avery. "You can cuddle with the mayor tonight. He loves Christmas. Lily Rock celebrates his birthday, you know. He came as a puppy two years ago. I'll tell you the whole story."

"Whatever," mumbled Avery.

Sage opened the doors of the truck as the elves hurried inside. She pulled her coat around her, feeling the cold slipping down her neck. "I need to dig out my wool scarf," she told them.

"If you stop by the dorm we can get out of these elf outfits," Avery suggested from the back seat.

"Will do. Don't take too long. There's a lot of work to be done."

28

PAWS AND PINES

Sage McCloud

Sage had a funny feeling as she pulled into the driveway. She'd been so busy with Thorny in the hospital and the elves, she'd forgotten to check in on Sparkles. Turning to the back seat, where Logan and Avery huddled in jackets and scarves, she asked, "Have either of you been to the shelter to see Sparkles lately?"

"I haven't," Logan said immediately. "I've been so busy with Wrap It Up!. But you have to ask her." He glared at Avery.

"I went over with Brad a couple of days ago," Avery admitted. "Sparkles was really edgy. She wouldn't let us near her."

Sage blinked. "Okay then, I'll check on her once you two start the baking. And then what do you think about inviting Justin over for Christmas?"

"I haven't seen him either," Logan said.

"I don't care if you invite Justin. But what about Sparkles? Ponies have feelings, right?" Avery looked to Sage for confirmation.

Surprised at Avery's preference, Sage asked, "I suppose ponies can feel lonely on Christmas. I guess I never thought of that."

"That's what I meant," said Avery.

Sage continued. "First I'll have a talk with Justin and invite him to Christmas breakfast. No one can resist Meadow's cinnamon rolls. Even if he's never had one, he must have heard about them."

When Avery's bottom lip quivered she added, "And we'll check on Sparkles later, if you'd like."

"I would like that a lot," Avery agreed.

It was Logan's turn to soothe Avery's feelings. "I don't know about ponies, but I do know that just the smell of cinnamon makes my mouth water." He changed the subject with a quick glance at Avery to see if his tactic worked. "I love the smell of cinnamon," he repeated.

And then he raised his arms into the air as if to stretch. Lowering his right arm, casually placing it around Avery's shoulders.

Now that's a boyfriend move I remember. Sage repressed a smile. To her surprise Avery didn't pull away. In fact, she leaned closer into Logan's side.

"Hurry up. It's cold," she mumbled.

Sage turned back toward the steering wheel. *Teenagers. It looks like there may be some romance in the air after all.* Before she could start the engine, she felt a tap on her shoulder. "I forgot my hat. Be right back," Logan said.

"I'll help you find it," Avery added.

Both were out of the door before Sage could object.

.   .   .

When the teens returned, Logan held the door for Avery and she hopped in first. He pulled the door closed, right when Sage noticed... *I think that's a bit of lip gloss around his mouth. And I don't see any hat.*

"We're ready," he told Sage. And then he wiped the back of his hand across his lips with a slight grin.

"Bork," Mayor Maguire agreed from the passenger seat.

"So Paws and Pines it is." She backed her truck up. "What took you so long anyway?"

"These." Avery held up a paper bag. "We snatched apples and some carrots from the teacher's room refrigerator. No one was around. They were just going bad. That's not stealing, right?" She turned to Logan for confirmation.

"Nope. Just good sense," he assured her.

As she drove the winding road to the shelter, Sage smiled to herself. *If I'm not mistaken, he's won her over. Even appealed to her better nature. Avery was genuinely concerned about Sparkles too. That means a lot. That has to be a Christmas miracle.*

Ten minutes later Sage pulled into the parking lot behind the kennel. She reached across and opened the passenger door. Mayor Maguire leaped down to the pavement and then led the way.

"It's so quiet," Sage remarked. "I wonder who got duty on Christmas? Not a creature is stirring, not even a doggo." They stood in front of the entrance to the shelter. Sage knocked, but no one came to the door. "And no lights on inside either. Let's try the barn," she told the teens.

Inside the barn, Avery was the first to announce, "The ponies are gone!"

A low whinny came from the back stall. Avery hurried

closer. "It's Sparkles. She's the only one left." The pony stared, wide-eyed, her nostrils flared.

Sage came close, using a soothing voice. "Left behind, I see. But it's okay. We've got you. Settle down now."

The horse stamped her hoof in protest.

"Can we help?" Logan asked.

"Stay back," Sage warned. "She's unpredictable."

Sparkles called out, her whinny stretching to a cry.

"She looks thin," Avery said. "Like she hasn't eaten. Even thinner than a few days ago."

"This will take some time," she told the teens. "I'll inch closer step by step. If you can hand me carrots, I think I can offer her a bite. She may take one and that would be a hopeful sign."

The rustling of the paper sack met her ears. Sage moved forward, noting the swish of Sparkles's tail. The hair was matted. Even the hair along her flanks showed patches of skin. *She must have rubbed against the wood in her stall. She's a very anxious pony.*

"You need a makeover," Sage continued to use her calmest voice. Then she took another step closer.

"Here's the carrot." Logan handed the paper bag to Sage.

"That's more like it," she said calmly. "Look what we have here, Sparkles." She took another step forward, her hand held flat, the carrot dangling over the edge.

The pony lowered her head to nose Sage's hand. Sparkles stepped backward with the shake of her head.

So Sage took another step forward. "You know you want the carrot," she coaxed. "Come on, Miss Obstinate, take a bite."

Sage kept her eyes on Sparkles. The pony stamped her hoof on the straw. She looked down, her tangled mane falling forward. When she raised her head, her eyes had softened.

Her hand still extended, Sage watched as Sparkles stretched her nose forward again to sniff the carrot. Sparkles nickered and then took the carrot, her teeth slowly chomping in appreciation.

29

ABANDONED AT CHRISTMAS

Sage McCloud

Once Sparkles began to readily take carrots from her hand, Sage sent Logan to search for anyone on duty at the shelter. As soon as he left the barn, Avery stepped closer, observing Sage with the skittish pony. "Can I brush her?" Avery asked. "Would she let me, you think?"

"I think a gentle grooming would be a great idea. Go over to that wall and see if you can find the brushes. And grab that tether. I'll clip it to her bridle. We'll have a better chance of keeping her calm," Sage directed.

By the time Logan returned, Avery stood at Sparkles's neck, combing her mane with long strokes. The horse reached for a mouthful of oats that Sage left in the trough. Sparkles lifted her head to nuzzle Avery's shoulder.

"Nobody around," Logan said. "The pony travel trailer's gone. Justin must have split before we got here." When he came closer to Avery, Sparkles shied away. "I just want to be friends," he told the horse.

"Once she gets used to you, you can braid her tail," Avery suggested with a shy grin. "She'd like that."

"I have no idea how to braid," Logan said.

"I'll teach you. Here, hold the comb."

Sage watched from a few feet away. *I'm so happy the elves are getting along.* Feeling confident that the pony had also turned a corner, she left them with Sparkles.

Now I have time to think about the kennel. The truth hit Sage in her gut. *With no one on duty and the place locked up, I need to check inside.*

Making her way across the dirt yard, she stopped at the front entrance of the shelter. Her stomach dropped. No sign of Brad. He'd been the one to take up shelter duty on Christmas Eve in the past. She pulled out her cell to text him.

I'm at P&P. No one here. Your job?

Not mine! Doc didn't tell me I am working tonight.

She could almost hear the exasperated tone in the text. *Brad feels nagged.* She felt that her constant surveillance may be making him impatient. She sent a thumbs-up emoji.

But that still doesn't solve my problem. I can't leave animals inside unsupervised. She held her cell in her hand and this time she texted her mother.

I'm at P&P. No one is here. Have to stay with Sparkles. Got Logan and Avery with me. Be home later.

Assuming her mother was elbow-deep in kneading her cinnamon rolls, Sage didn't expect a response. Pocketing her phone, she made her way back to the barn.

30

THE CINNAMON CHALLENGE

Meadow McCloud

Meadow shoved a paper across the desk toward Janis. "Here's information on the Baubles the Clown website. And here's the brother's phone number. Baubles's given name is Robert Abernathy."

Janis took the papers. With a quick read, she turned toward her computer. "I let this drop," she admitted. "I thought forensics would report back sooner. Probably a delay because of the holidays. I should have known better. Only myself to blame."

Hands held aloft, she stared at her computer. "Okay, I'm looking right here at the Baubles the Clown website. I can see the photos of birthday parties." She turned to Meadow. "You make a pretty good detective, the way you found the names of the people who hired him. Nice work." Meadow had to admit even a half-hearted compliment from Janis made her feel slightly pleased.

"I would have come in sooner, but I didn't want to interfere," she said.

"You'd be the first," Janis commented dryly. "Everyone else in Lily Rock thinks being a detective is their part-time gig. You wouldn't believe all the bad advice that comes my way. But you are different. Did you do a search using his real name?" Jets stared at her screen.

"I did, I searched for Robert Abernathy."

Janis smiled. "Good work. I'm under the impression he was paid in cash. I wish I had some influence when it comes to that."

"Yes, dear. Of course you're correct. Anyway once I got more info about Robert I came straight over to you," Meadow said demurely. "Like I said, I didn't want to interfere."

What Meadow didn't say was that she had to settle Thorny into her spare bedroom, get the sleeping bags out for the elves, and change Mayor Maguire's hat and collar for the Christmas tree lighting in the park. And there was also the cinnamon roll dough...

The list rolled in her head, making her feel more and more anxious. *There's not enough time for me to get this done. I haven't finished baking cookies nor made the deliveries. People will be dropping in all day tomorrow.* She wrung her hands in her lap.

"Well this is pretty interesting," Jets turned from her computer. "It seems Mr. Abernathy has a past. One I'd never considered."

"What do you mean?" Meadow leaned forward.

"He was at Stanford. And while he was there he became quite the internet sensation, from what I can tell. He single-handedly dominated a very popular practice with teens. What some people called the cinnamon challenge."

"A baking contest?" Meadow could hardly believe her ears.

"Not really," Jets pointed at her screen. "Come around the desk and have a look."

"What was he thinking?" Meadow had resumed her chair on the other side of Janis's desk.

"College kids do stupid things," Jets said.

"But he was a smart college student. Accepted into Stanford. Not like Brad, wandering around aimlessly, looking for trouble."

"I suppose his cinnamon challenge sounded innocent enough at first. Eating spoonfuls of the stuff. His pals timed it for sixty seconds. And then the other stipulation. You couldn't drink any liquid."

Meadow shook her head. "Did he think it was like a hot dog eating contest? Other than a passion for carcinogen-infused meat products, that's the only reason why someone would try such nonsense."

"No, he was a crazy college kid who was avoiding his studies and just wanted attention. The videos were eventually shut down because some kids were taken to the emergency room. No one died, but I think there was a boy with a previous condition who went into a coma." Janis kept clicking. "You might not know it, but cinnamon residue comes from tree bark, covers the throat and lungs and makes it difficult to breathe. When the kid went into a coma, parents finally complained about the challenges. They were shut down, at least for a time."

Jets's forehead wrinkled. "On the one hand I knew about this challenge somewhere in the back of my mind, but on the other hand I can't believe my case might be the fallout from something stupid that happened fifteen years ago."

Meadow felt fidgety. "How does this cinnamon nonsense connect with Baubles? Did I miss something?"

Janis tapped her fingers on her desk. "Now that this is getting very serious, I'm not sure how much to tell you. Confidentiality and all. But considering it's Christmas and how you got the evidence, I'm inclined to bend the rules."

"So start telling me what you know!" Meadow felt exasperated. She'd used valuable preparation time sharing her information with Janis. And now it was past dinner hour, and her to-do list wasn't getting any shorter.

"Let me do some more thinking," Jets said. "And I'll get back to you."

Meadow stood. "I have so much to do. Christmas is tomorrow. I hope you find your killer." She left with a huff.

31

CLEAN AND SOBER

Meadow McCloud

Meadow stood in her kitchen. Apron tied at the back of her waist, she finished rolling out the dough for the last batch of sugar cookies. Mayor Maguire stood by her side, attentively watching.

She tossed him a scrap, which he caught in the air and swallowed in one gulp. *Michael will be here very soon with Thorny. I have to stop baking and greet them. Everyone expects me to be in a good mood.*

Meadow reached for her cell phone, scrolled through her messages, and then slipped it back in the oversized apron pocket. *Nothing from Officer Jets.* The doorbell rang, followed by a sharp bark from Mayor Maguire.

In the living room she found Michael had let himself inside. He held a sleeping bag under one arm and a back-pack hung from his hand. "We picked up some clothes for Thorny. You wouldn't believe the mess in his house. It's going to need a bulldozer to tidy up for him before he goes back. I couldn't even find his jacket and he had no clue where it might be."

Meadow looked over Michael's shoulder, expecting to see Thorny. He caught her glance. "I left our patient with the heat on in the truck while I started grabbing a few things from the garage. As soon as I make one more trip, I'll help Thorny out of the truck and I'll start a fire. You want this stuff over there?" He nodded toward the hearth.

Tears came to her eyes. "Oh, Michael. You are a Christmas angel. Yes, put them over there and bring in the honored guest. Is he doing okay?"

"Not sure," Michael mumbled. "But when he smells the sugar cookies and sits close to the fire, I think he'll perk right up." Michael dropped the sleeping bag and closed the door behind him.

When he returned he wore a stocking hat pulled over his ears and carried a duffle bag in one hand. "This is Thorny's change of clothes. I think it's going to snow for the Christmas tree lighting. We'd better bundle up," he cautioned.

By the time she'd pulled an easy chair closer to the hearth, the door opened again. Thorny entered with a burst of cold air. Michael followed.

"Bork." Mayor Maguire ran toward Thorny to poke his knee. Then he sat down to offer a paw.

"Don't you ever feed this mutt?" Thorny asked in a gruff voice.

"About every five minutes," Meadow chuckled. "Come sit down, dear. We're all ready for you. Right over here." She patted the back of the chair. "You can watch as Michael builds a fire. I planned to have it going before you got here but..."

Meadow wanted to add that life intervened, but she

didn't think that in his condition, Thornton would appreciate her small problems. Especially when compared to his.

"I'd like to wash up first, if you don't mind?" Thornton looked around the room. Then he bent down to give Maguire a pat.

"I have you all set up for the guest room. Come this way." Meadow bustled down the hall, carrying the overnight bag. She began to admonish herself. *I planned to have the guest room all ready but didn't get to it. I still need to put the sheets on the bed and set out towels. How will I manage...* Her nerves got the better of her again. Despite all of Michael's help, she felt extremely scattered. Not like her usual organized self.

"Mom, I'm home," Sage called from the living room. "With the elves," she added.

Now we're all here. Meadow sighed. *Do I go back to the living room or get Thornton's room ready?*

Voices coming from the front of the house helped her decide. Sage must have said something funny to Thorny, because she could hear his gravelly laugh. *While they chat I can make the bed,* Meadow thought. *And get out some towels. And fluff the comforter. And pull the curtains to keep out the cold.*

Once she'd finished with her preparations, Meadow returned to the living room. To her surprise, Avery was speaking animatedly about Sparkles.

"So Ms. McCloud kept taking slow steps toward the pony. She'd pause and then offer a bite of carrot. Then she'd do it again, getting closer and closer. Pretty soon she got close enough to pat Sparkles on her neck. By the time Ms. McCloud was done, I was brushing Sparkles's mane, Logan braided her tail, while Sparkles kept nosing me for more food."

Avery's face glowed. Meadow couldn't help but notice how different she sounded, her voice lively and interested. *This isn't the first time a pony has captured the heart of a young girl*, Meadow thought. "Did you bring Sparkles with you?" She kept her face serious.

"Mom," Sage cried. "I think we already have a full house. Sparkles will be fine in the barn. We cinched a coat on her and bedded her down with lots of straw. Even if the temperature drops she'll be fine."

"I'll check on her tomorrow morning," Avery broke in. "So she won't feel left out. It's Christmas."

Apparently underneath all of Avery's cynicism, there was a tender heart. *Who knew*, thought Meadow. *It took Sage to figure all of that out. I'm so proud of her.* Meadow's eyes filled with tears. She brushed them away before anyone could see. "I need to get some dough rising," she commented over her shoulder.

"Do you want help?" Logan offered. "I want to learn to bake, if it's not too much trouble."

Meadow put her hands on her hips. "What's come over you two?" She stared at Avery and Logan. "Talk about a change in attitude."

Logan shot Avery a quick glance. Then they both giggled.

So that's it, Meadow realized. Avery and Logan had finally connected.

Standing beside Meadow at the counter, Logan reached for the recipe printed on a 3x5 card. It was covered in small scribbles, front and back. "This looks old," he commented.

"It was my mother's recipe," Meadow said. "She had a special way with raised dough. Treated each batch individually. It took me years to learn her touch, the way she kneaded and then let the dough rest.

"I don't think I've ever baked a batch of cinnamon rolls quite as good as hers," Meadow continued. "But I keep trying." She smiled at Logan. "You could use an apron; I have a clean one in that bottom drawer."

32

ANOTHER PHONE CALL

Meadow McCloud

By the time Thornton was settled into the guest room, Meadow returned to the kitchen to instruct Logan. She left him to work on his kneading technique so that she could warm herself by the fire. She found Avery sitting in a chair, staring out the window. "I hope it snows," the girl said wistfully.

It's easy to feel melancholy when you're alone, staring into the dark. "Avery, dear, would you mind helping Logan in the kitchen? He could use some assistance with the cinnamon rolls." Meadow was rewarded with a huge smile.

"Mom?" Sage called from down the hall. "What happened to Mike—isn't he supposed to be here?"

"He went home to get a warm jacket for Thornton," Meadow explained. When Sage came closer, she noted a worried look on her daughter's face. "Is everything all right?"

Meadow sat on one end of the oversized sofa. She patted the cushion next to her.

"I sent you a text..." Sage sat down and then curled her legs up underneath her body. "There's no one at Paws and Pines to look after the animals. Sparkles is alone and I didn't hear any barking from the kennels. I'm worried."

Meadow couldn't imagine the doc would abandon his favorite project. "Did you call Doc?" she asked.

"First I texted and then I left him three voicemails." Sage twisted the end of her braid in her hand. "He hasn't responded yet. I suppose we'll see him at the tree lighting."

"What about Brad?" Meadow asked. "He may know more."

"He said he wasn't supposed to work tonight. Should I call him back and ask him to go over anyway?"

"Not a terrible idea," Meadow nodded. "He's never attended the tree lighting in the past. We can swing by afterward to check on him. Bring a plate of cookies. Make sure he's coming over tomorrow." Meadow sat back, folding her hands in her lap. "I worry about that boy. It can get lonely this time of year. As much as I'm concerned for the animals, I'm even more concerned about him."

Sage nodded in agreement. "Ever since we started talking, Brad's become my personal project. I ignored him for a long time, thinking he just needed to, you know, grow up. He's a hard worker but he's taking the wrong jobs; I used to think Paws and Pines would be a good influence." She looked away and then continued. "I want to have a word with Doc. I don't think he sees what I see with Brad."

Meadow felt her heart beat against her chest. The usual tone of confidence when she spoke of the doc was missing from Sage's voice. *She's begun to doubt.*

Sage continued to explain. "Brad just told me that the doc sent him to go through Baubles's room. The doc was worried the cops would find weed at the shelter. He especially didn't want that discovery landing back on him. I guess there's some kind of investigation going on...

"Of course Brad was terrified. He'd never say he was, but I could see it in his face. Once he's afraid, he acts impulsively.

"And to make matters worse, Brad stole something from Baubles's room. A wooden box with some weed and papers. I told him he had to turn it over to the constabulary. I even went with him. And wouldn't you know, Janis found menacing notes on papers hidden underneath a false bottom right in the box."

Meadow shuddered. "Menacing notes?"

"That's right."

"So someone was threatening Baubles?" Meadow said under her breath. *I bet that's what Janis didn't want to tell me earlier.*

Before Sage could say more, the now familiar intrusive thought popped into Meadow's mind. *Is this the time? Do I tell her now about the doc and her adoption?* It seemed nearly every conversation with her daughter as of late ended up with her wondering the same thing.

Clearing her throat, Meadow began to speak, interrupted by her cell buzzing in her apron pocket. "I have to take this!" she explained to Sage. She smiled at the prompt on her screen and stood.

"It's a FaceTime call. I need to get Thorny." Hurrying down the hall, she knocked on the bedroom door. "Thornton, dear. I have a call for you."

When he opened the door, she nodded her approval at his changed appearance. His hair, tousled and combed back, smelled of pine shampoo. He'd put on an old wool sweater with clean worn jeans. "What's going on?" he asked.

She handed him the phone. "Someone wants to wish you a Merry Christmas."

Thornton's face dropped. He took the cell and held it up.

"Hey, sweetie," Meadow heard Robyn's voice say. "Meadow tells me you're staying with her for a few days. I miss you so much."

Thornton's chin began to tremble. Tears formed in his eyes. One glance at Meadow and he burst into sobs, words catching in his throat. "Hey, babe," was all he could get out, overcome with emotion.

Meadow lifted the corner of her apron to help pat his face.

"I've been wanting to call you," Thornton explained. "But I lost my phone..." He turned away from Meadow, closing the door with his other hand.

Aware that Sage stood behind her, Meadow turned to face her daughter.

"Mom, what did you do?" Sage asked.

"I contacted the security facility where Robyn is staying and arranged a FaceTime call. I only recently realized that Thorny had lost his phone. So he hadn't been able to call her for several weeks. And because he's proud, he never asked for help."

Sage reached her arms around her mother's waist. She buried her face into her neck, hugging her close. "You are such a good person. I hope I become half as caring as you."

Meadow wrapped her arms around her daughter. *I only hope you'll still think that when I tell you how I've lied all these years.* She couldn't let herself off the hook. Not yet, not until her secret was shared.

As she held Sage close, Meadow realized something new. Maybe she wasn't ready to tell Sage about her adoption, but that wasn't the point really, her readiness. The truth was that Sage was more than ready to hear what she had to say. Sage was a mature loving woman now. She required the truth to move forward with her beautiful life.

33

LILY ROCK RUMORS

Sage McCloud

Am I doing the right thing? Sage sat in her truck thinking about the conversation with Meadow earlier. She'd felt unsettled. *It's as if Meadow is holding back something...*

Used to her mother's candidness, Sage felt the disconnect strongly and wondered if she'd done something wrong. "Take a fearless moral inventory," Meadow used to tell her whenever she brought her a problem.

But try as she may, Sage couldn't think of anything that had caused Meadow to pull back. *Everything seems a bit off-kilter this year*, Sage concluded.

Her thoughts returned to their houseguests. Logan and Avery seemed to be having a wonderful time baking. Michael was so much calmer this year. *That's a good thing. I'm overreacting*, Sage thought. *Don't forget the holiday hubbub and the teasing and good baking smells. Focus on the happy moments.* She took a deep breath. *But what about*

Sparkles? All alone in that barn without the other ponies to keep her company.

I'm not going to leave Sparkles by herself for Christmas.

When Sage arrived at the shelter, she found Brad's truck in the parking lot. A glimmer of light behind the reception counter made her look inside. But no sight of Brad. So she pulled out her phone.

I'm at the shelter. Out front.

She waited but didn't get a response.

After a search around the shelter, she made her way to the barn to find Brad sitting in the corner of Sparkles's stall, his chin resting on pulled-up knees.

"Hey, Brad."

He lifted his head. "Hey yourself." Dressed in a thick denim jacket and a soft plaid scarf, he looked younger and sadly vulnerable. Sage stepped closer. He met her gaze, adding a slight smile.

"I thought you'd be at the reception counter."

A soft neigh came from Sparkles. Sage walked closer to give her a pat.

"Are you keeping her company? It must be working, she's still nice and calm. That's good."

"Oh yeah, we're best friends now." Brad stood up, brushing the straw off his jeans. "What happened to the other ponies?"

"Justin took them down the hill. He left Sparkles behind," Sage admitted.

"Did he steal them? I thought they belonged to Baubles."

Sage shrugged. "I never thought of that. I suppose after Christmas Janis will have another problem to solve. The case of the missing ponies."

"I guess," Brad said. Then he patted Sparkles's neck. "Somebody combed her. She looks ready for Christmas." Brad reached out an open palm and offered a carrot to Sparkles. The pony took it in her mouth and began to chomp.

"Are you staying here all night?" Sage asked.

"The doc said I could."

"Why not inside? Somebody has to watch the dogs and cats."

"They've been removed." Brad's voice dropped. "I guess the shelter will be shut down. Doc was really mad. Told me he was being unfairly persecuted."

"Unfairly persecuted..." Sage wondered aloud. "It was my understanding that the doc has a wonderful reputation and is loved by everyone. At least that's what I've always been told by my mom." She stopped and then added, "And others in Lily Rock."

"I guess." Brad sounded vague.

Am I becoming paranoid, or is this the second time I feel like people close to me are withholding information? "So have you heard otherwise about Doc?" Sage insisted.

"Kind of," he admitted. "There are rumors."

"What kind of rumors?"

"That the doc controls Skye and other people in town. He has embarrassing information on them and threatens them if they don't do what he wants."

"Blackmail?" Sage felt her gut clench.

"Not for money so much as..." Brad hesitated. "Requests. He asks people to do things for him, awkward things." Brad shifted from one foot to the other. "You know he works at the women's clinic?"

"Oh, I've heard that!" Sage exclaimed. "Doc helps out with adoptions. His office is open to women with unwanted pregnancies. He makes sure they get counseling."

Brad's face fell. He just stared at Sage, shoving his hands into his pockets.

He's not saying everything he knows. Sage probed further. "So who else in Lily Rock? You mentioned Skye. My mother. Does the doc have something on her?"

He stepped back. "I don't know what, but there are rumors. I hear things." Then he shrugged. "But really, I forget a lot too. I'm thinking you might be right, that smoking so much weed is making me lose my memory."

Sage realized this was her chance since he'd brought it up. "It does do that, or so I've heard. So you're trying to cut back?"

"I already have," Brad admitted. "Just look at Thorny. He's a mess. With the drinking and me supplying him. I don't give him that much but I don't think it's good for him either."

A snort came from the stall. Sparkles shook her head. Then she stamped her hoof.

"Not to change the subject," Brad began, "but did you ever see that old TV show, *Mr. Ed?*"

Sage took a breath of relief. She welcomed a change of topic. "I used to watch that show all the time. With Wilbur and his talking horse. That one, right?"

"Well it may have been the weed..." Brad scratched behind his ear. "But I could swear Sparkles was talking to me right before you arrived."

"No way!" Sage began to giggle.

"It wasn't the voice of Mr. Ed. Not like that. It was kind of cultured. Snooty almost."

Sage knew that Brad was trying to cheer her up, with a

story about a talking horse. But instead of resisting, she went along. "So what did Sparkles have to say exactly?"

"She wants to go to the tree lighting," he explained carefully.

When he was so serious, Sage burst out laughing. "You've got to be..."

Then she stopped herself. Had she and Meadow not just said that Brad needed more company? And that he usually stayed away from the holiday festivities? Maybe this was Brad's way of saying he wanted to be included.

She reached for Sparkles's bridle off the wall. "I refuse to be the person to dismiss a talking pony. Let's saddle her up and walk her into town."

"Really, you'd do that?" Brad's smile was her reward.

"Come on, we only have an hour. I know a path through the woods that leads directly into Lily Rock. It will be beautiful. Grab your flashlight and we'll get going."

For the second time, Sage burst out laughing at Brad's surprised expression. "Who carries a flashlight with them?"

"Never mind. Turn on your cell phone light. That will do the trick."

34

THROUGH THE WOODS

Sage McCloud

"I never knew about this path." Brad held his phone up high so the light would illuminate the way for Sage and Sparkles.

"This was my secret trail when I was younger." Sage tugged on Sparkles's lead to pull her head up from munching a weed. "Not now," Sage coaxed the horse.

Was it only earlier that day when Sparkles refused to eat? And now she wouldn't stop. She clucked her tongue to urge the pony forward. In the darkness, a hawk swept past her head, careening to the next tree.

"I've known about this shortcut to town since I was quite young," Sage explained. "I spent hours at the stables. Then I'd sprint on this path and meet Mom at the library. It only takes ten minutes this way."

"Good to know," Brad called over his shoulder.

"Caw, caw," echoed in the night air. Brad ducked. "What was that?"

"Crows," Sage explained. "I thought you'd be more in touch with nature, living in Lily Rock all these years."

He lowered his cell phone light, turning toward her. "I was kinda busy. Never got into the hiking things some guys do up here. I've never been on the Lily Rock trail, for example."

"Have you ridden a horse?" Sage asked.

"Nope."

"So let's change a few things. You're not alone at the shelter for the tree lighting, for one. Afterward, why don't you come over Christmas morning? Stay as long as you like."

Brad turned back around, holding up his light. "Is Avery going to be there?" he asked, sounding hopeful. "I was hoping to find her at the barn. That's why I ended up with Sparkles."

"You like Avery a lot," Sage commented.

"She's really hot," Brad admitted. "And she's only here until June. So I thought we could hang out until then."

Sage wasn't sure what to say. Avery and Logan seemed to have found each other and she didn't want to get in the middle of a love triangle. Maybe Brad would have a chance once Logan left.

But for now Sage wanted Brad to be with friends at Christmas. She clicked her tongue again, urging the pony to move faster.

With a shake of her head, Sparkles broke into a trot. Pushing past Brad, Sage managed to pull her back. "Whoa," she said.

Brad jogged closer, reaching to pat the pony's neck. "I like the way her mane is braided with the ribbons. Meadow will think that's cool." He tugged on one to straighten it out. "How much longer until we reach town?" he asked, turning to Sage.

"'Five minutes or so. I wanted to know something else." Sage cleared her throat.

"What's that?" Brad asked.

"On the day Baubles was murdered, did you witness anything unusual?" Even in the dark she could see his shoulders tense.

"I was there," he said slowly. "I didn't tell anyone because..."

"You were protecting someone else," Sage interjected. It only took a moment for her to guess. "Was it Thorny? Was he in the barn too?"

Brad shrugged. "I walked in, you know, to deliver some product, and I saw him with the body. Baubles was slumped in front of the pony and Thorny was looking at the rope around his neck."

"Did you speak to Thorny? Ask him what happened?"

"No, I was afraid I'd get in trouble. Plus I didn't want to narc on him. I thought maybe Thorny and Baubles got into some kind of a fight. It was so weird, a clown slumped against Sparkles's leg that way." Brad shuddered.

"Did Thorny see you?" Sage felt her heart beat faster.

"He must have heard something because he turned to look around. I could see his face from where I was hiding. I think he might have been crying. Then he looked down and saw something in the straw. He leaned over and picked it up."

"What kind of something?"

"I still can't believe this, but it looked like one of those metal straws. I kept watching to see what he'd do with it. Thorny slid it into his pocket. Then he walked outside, so I left the other way. I musta been pretty high. It probably wasn't a metal straw."

Sage didn't disagree with Brad. But she still wasn't sure

if he was using Thorny as an excuse, maybe casting the blame on him just to cover for himself. "You have any issues with Baubles?" She did her best to sound calm.

"Not me," Brad said quickly. "He was a customer, that's all. An odd guy, with his face paint and everything."

Sage stopped asking questions after that. She pointed to the distance, where light shone between the trees. "It's Lily Rock," she told him. "Quite a crowd."

Brad clicked his cell light off.

35

MISTAKEN IDENTITIES

Sage McCloud

Emerging from the woods, Sage smiled at the people congregating in the park. The creche had been lit to allow children to approach and touch the statues. Mayor Maguire stood near the baby Jesus, offering a paw of welcome.

"Aren't the trees supposed to be lit up?" Brad asked.

"Not until nine o'clock. The Old Rockers are nothing if not punctual. I think we made it in time." And then to Sage's surprise, the voices dropped off as the crowd, one by one, turned to stare in their direction.

A child announced in a high-pitched tone, "Look, Mommy. It's Mary and Joseph and the donkey."

Sage suppressed a smile. Every year something surprised her on Christmas Eve. But she'd never been mistaken for the Virgin Mary before. *That's a first...*

Brad stepped closer to ask, "What's she talking about?"

That stunned Sage. Apparently Brad wasn't very familiar with the story.

"You know. She thinks we're like Joseph and Mary coming into Bethlehem, looking for a place to stay. And then Jesus is born in a barn called a manger. It's in the Bible."

"Oh," Brad said, for once short on words. "I guess I saw that on TV when I was little. *A Charlie Brown Christmas...*"

Sage patted Sparkles's neck. "Right. I love that show. Let's go," she said, clucking her tongue at Sparkles. The pony trotted forward, Brad running alongside to keep up.

36

"THANKS, MISS MARPLE"

Meadow McCloud

Earlier that evening Meadow sat on the edge of Thornton's bed. She'd settled him in with a mug of spicy herbal tea to help him sleep. "So did you and Robyn have a good chat?" She pulled the comforter up to his chin.

Tears filled his eyes. "I've been crying like a baby all evening," he admitted.

"That's just love, dear. Nothing to worry about." She adjusted the comforter, adding a couple of pats.

"Being sober hurts," he muttered. "It's only been a couple of days. You sure I can't have a little nip to get me past Christmas?" Meadow knew he only asked to be told no. She'd learned that the hard way.

"No, dear. You cannot have a little nip. Just tea for now. I bet you'll fall right to sleep in no time. But Thorny, I have a question for you."

"What's that?" he mumbled, his voice already growing drowsy.

"What happened to that metal straw, the one you've been carrying in your pocket all week?"

"What straw do you mean?" His eyelids drifted shut.

Meadow grew impatient. She knew that straw was important and she wanted to shake him awake. But then a voice called from the other room.

"Time to go to the tree lighting," Michael announced. "Truck's warmed up."

"Be right there," she called back. Turning to Thorny, she hoped her loud response would have stirred him awake. But she could see right away that she wasn't getting any more information out of him tonight. There was a gurgle and then a loud snore; he'd dropped off to sleep.

As she went to grab her jacket out of her room, she reminded herself to stop being impatient. Sometimes the early days of sobriety brought on a lot of sleep, if for no other reason than not to feel the need for alcohol. Plus sleep was what Thornton needed to recover. Not dragging him to see the Christmas lights might have been more kind than forcing him to go. Plus there was always next year.

On the drive into town, Meadow glanced to the back seat. Logan and Avery held hands, snuggling close together. She turned back to speak to Michael. "I didn't get my cinnamon rolls in the oven," she told him.

"I can help you later, when we get back from the tree lighting." He glanced at the rearview mirror. "It seems Elf One and Elf Two have something else on their minds."

"I suppose they left a mess in my kitchen," Meadow groaned.

"Don't worry." Michael deftly turned the steering wheel into a curve. "Like I said, I can help. Sage can help. Maybe we can train ol' Thorny to lend a hand tomorrow morning. This isn't entirely on your shoulders, you know, making Christmas happen."

She admitted that Michael sounded reasonable, but she knew differently. Without her, none of Christmas would have happened over the years. She felt certain of that. With a sigh she changed the subject. "Where's Marla this evening?"

"At her house. I'm worried about her," Michael admitted. "She's not been feeling well for months. Not even Christmas is getting her out of the house."

"Can't we go by and just oust her in her pajamas?" Other than Thorny, who was an exception this year, Meadow didn't like people to pass on the holiday entirely. Even if they weren't religious, they could get a bit of cheer from the decorations and good spirits of others.

"She's not having that. I've tried before. But she has been talking about inviting an old high school friend of hers up for a visit." Michael sounded more hopeful. "I think that's a good idea."

"Do you know this person?" Meadow asked.

"I don't." His curt response made her curious.

When he didn't elaborate, she poked him a bit more. "Do you want to know this person? Is she female, perchance?"

"She's a young woman. Around Sage's age." Michael pulled his truck into a parking space. Then he quickly changed the subject. "I can't believe I found a spot right behind the constabulary. Hop on out, everyone."

Across the street people ambled around the booths, talking and greeting friends and neighbors. Several children held oversized gingerbread cookies. Most of the adults sipped steaming beverages from small ceramic mugs with a photo of Mayor Maguire in his Christmas hat printed on the side.

"Thorny missed all this." Meadow felt a tinge of sadness.

"You did the right thing." Michael patted her shoulder. "If you're worried, I can go check on him later."

"I don't know what we ever did without you." Meadow wrapped an arm around his waist and gave him a squeeze.

"Lily Rock is home," he stated. "You and Sage made it that way for me."

Meadow scanned the crowd, then glanced back toward the library. "Would you excuse me for a few minutes? I have something to check on. I'll be right back." She dropped her arm from around Michael's waist and stepped across the street.

I've been so worried about Thorny I forgot about my research. Janis is paying attention to Baubles, but has she looked into Justin? It will only take a few minutes, and then I can be back for the tree lighting.

Once at her computer, she typed in Justin Young. Narrowing down the options took little time. She found the right Justin on a social media account. He stood next to a hospital bed.

A teenage boy, a respirator mask over his face, lay in the bed. The teen's eyes were closed, his body looked thin underneath the sheets. A few words told the story.

She read the caption under the photo: "He's still in a coma. Can't breathe on his own."

Meadow scrolled through the posts, finding a photo for the same time every year. "Happy birthday, son. We hope you'll be awake to celebrate next year."

Pausing on each post, she traced how over the years, the

boy was not improving. He lay as if asleep, hooked up to machines. The posts had become less and less optimistic. The final one made Meadow's heart break. "James is gone. My darling boy."

Meadow made note of the date of the last post, only six months ago. Then she copied a link before closing her screen. *Maybe Officer Jets already knows, but maybe she doesn't. I need to show her this right now.*

After locking the library, Meadow made her way back across the street. She pulled out her cell phone to text Janis the information and paste the link. But before she could press Send, a familiar voice interrupted.

"If it isn't the queen of Christmas, Meadow McCloud. A merry ho, ho, ho to you." Instead of sounding cheery, the voice held a rasp of sarcasm.

Doc May wore a quilted coat. The fur around the collar looked authentic. Before she could say hello, the doc kept speaking.

"So they closed me down. You left some evidence. I guess you already knew that?" His accusatory tone made Meadow flinch. He continued to detail her inefficiency.

"I told you all of the CBD should be gone. And yet they found enough at the reception desk to take the dogs and cats and close my doors. Who knows what they did with them on Christmas Eve. I know we have you to thank for such carelessness, now don't we."

Despite the cold, Meadow felt perspiration break out on the palms of her hands. This wasn't the first time the doc had played on her sensitive heart to make her feel guilty. She'd grown to expect his harsh words when things didn't go quite his way.

But this time, especially when she was trying so hard at

Christmas, it hurt more. Over the months she'd changed her mind about him as a person, realizing he wasn't the man she thought he was. *He managed to manipulate me all of those years. So that I've kept the truth from Sage. And maybe made her life less than it could be.*

So now, despite her fear, instead of doing what she always did, which was to placate and make excuses, she set her jaw firmly and stared him right in the eye. Her moist hand gripped into a fist. "Closing down Paws and Pines is not my fault. It's solely on your shoulders. Using animals to test your theories about CBD isn't legal. You're not a veterinarian. You have no license to do so."

The shock on his face made Meadow's knees shake. Instead of waiting for him to deride her further, she took matters into her own hands. Meadow left the doc standing on the boardwalk as she strode across the street.

With a deep breath she released her fist, shoving each hand into a worn glove. Spotting Sage standing alongside Sparkles, Meadow noticed a child sitting on the saddle. Others waited in line for a turn.

"She seems recovered," Meadow said, pointing to the Shetland, her voice still shaking from her encounter with the doc.

Sage nodded. "Look at all these children. Everyone thinks this is the donkey that Mary rode into Bethlehem. They all want a ride."

Meadow chuckled. *Now that's what Christmas is about. Those little surprises no one can plan for. They just happen.* Then she remembered. "I forgot to send a text," she explained to Sage. "Give me a minute."

Stepping aside, Meadow pulled out her phone. She added a few words and then pressed Send.

I've got information about Justin Young.
Here's the link.

Thanks, Miss Marple.

37

FULL HOUSE

Meadow McCloud

Early Christmas morning Meadow awoke to the ticking of her old alarm clock. She reached over to grab it and stare at the dial. *I'm late,* she realized with a start. *I thought I set it last night.*

But then she realized she had other things on her mind. Tucked into her bed with the light out, all of the chores she'd not been able to accomplish before Christmas stacked up in her head, just like dirty plates next to the sink. But then she rolled over and put everything out of her mind. *I can't deal with this now.*

Placing her alarm back on the nightstand, she fell back onto the pillow. *It's Christmas, and who knows if there will be cinnamon rolls. I'd better get up.* Meadow pulled on her worn slippers and flannel bathrobe. She sniffed. *I smell cinnamon,* she thought. *And coffee.*

After brushing her hair, she hurried down the hall. The

fire crackled in the living room with Logan and Avery snuggled in their sleeping bags, fast asleep. And right next to them was Brad, huddled in a quilt with a stocking cap pulled over his ears.

Quiet laughter caught her attention. Following the voices into the kitchen, she found Michael and Sage. He was the first to say, "Merry Christmas!"

He held his finger over his lips, nodding toward the living room. "We're letting the elves sleep in."

Sage came closer to give her a kiss on the cheek. She pointed to a plate and mug that were set on a red Christmas placemat at her usual place at the table.

Meadow felt confused. "I need to get baking," she told them.

"Nope. Me and Mike have got this. Just have a seat." Sage pulled out her chair.

"Mike and I, dear." Meadow couldn't help but correct Sage.

Sage laughed and then filled Meadow's mug with fresh coffee.

"I've got one batch of cinnamon rolls out of the oven. And another rising over there." Sage pointed to the old batter bowl in the corner. "Not as good as yours, of course, but I hope to improve each year."

Sage placed a roll on Meadow's plate. White frosting oozed over the sides. A few raisins peeked out from the dough. The snail shape wasn't quite even, but like Sage said, she'd learn.

"This looks yummy, dear." Meadow reached for her fork, expertly cutting away the first bite. Michael and Sage watched as she politely chewed and then swallowed. A small smile came to the corners of her lips. "Oh, delicious.

Certainly better than any of my first attempts. A little more nutmeg next time and you are well on your way."

A sigh of relief escaped from Michael. "We were up late with the elves. They made a big mess, but we settled them to sleep and then got to work in earnest." Meadow caught his happy expression, feeling her heart warm. She remembered how different he was the year before. She reached to pat his hand.

"Did you get any sleep?"

"I got enough." He smiled. "I sent Sage to bed around one o'clock and cleaned up the kitchen. I wasn't having you doing dishes on Christmas morning."

"I see." Meadow lifted her mug. A feeling of contentment replaced her initial anxiety. She hadn't felt this way in a long time. In fact, it had been so long, she'd forgotten the possibility.

Another sip of coffee made her realize—her daughter had taken Christmas into her own hands this year. She'd decorated and baked. And she'd found time to thrill the onlookers, being mistaken for Mary leading Sparkles. And she'd helped Brad through a difficult time. She'd even decorated the house and tree. Pride and love filled Meadow's heart.

Before she could thank Michael and Sage, a voice from the living room called, "Is that cinnamon rolls I smell?" Logan, wearing sweatpants and a Lily Rock Music Academy sweatshirt, stood in the doorway.

"Go brush your teeth," Sage said sternly. "Then I'll have breakfast all ready."

38

SOMEBODY'S KNOCKING AT
THE DOOR

Meadow McCloud

"I'll get that." Michael rose to answer the door from the other room.

"I'm here to see Miss Marple," came the demanding voice of Janis Jets.

"It's seven o'clock in the morning. Don't you ever rest?" Michael closed the door behind her. "I assume you mean Meadow...we're in the kitchen.

Sage immediately set another place for Janis, who strode into the kitchen looking skeptically at the table. "All fluffed up for Santa," she said tartly. "I can't wait for this time of year to be over."

"Sit down and have a cinnamon roll. Sage and I made them." The sound of pride in Michael's voice made Meadow smirk.

"Oh, okay. I guess I am hungry." Jets plopped herself down at the table.

Sage put the roll in front of her. Janis snatched a fork. Then she put it down and pulled at the roll with her fingers instead. Two huge bites later, she took a sip of coffee. "Not bad. Not like Meadow's, but pretty good." Janis sounded impressed.

Meadow felt herself blush at the compliment. But then she checked herself. Surely Janis's arrival wasn't a coincidence. "You showing up this early on Christmas," she said tartly. "This feels like a business call."

"I sent your link to our team last night," Janis explained to Meadow. "And I have to tell you, this is the perfect Christmas, my favorite so far in Lily Rock. One in a million because I arrested a murderer on Christmas Eve while all the rest of you were drinking hot chocolate and playing kissy poo." She glared at Logan, who looked away as he tried to hide a guilty grin.

Meadow leaned forward with interest. But it was Sage who spoke first. "No one's allowed to talk about murderers on Christmas morning. It's a rule."

"Whose rule?" Jets looked skeptical.

"Mom's. She told me Christmas was a special day, filled with surprises and joy. That's the way it's been my whole life!"

"I'd like to amend my previous statement," Meadow stated clearly. "Christmas is special all on its own. We don't have to bury real life to give it any more joy than it already contains." She turned to Jets. "So tell us everything. I want to know!"

Sage sat down, a look of mystification on her face.

"Miss Marple, I knew you were on my side," Jets agreed. "Give me a sec. I left my laptop in the truck." On her feet, she licked icing from the corner of her mouth.

Then she nodded at Sage. "Could you move that pony

out of my way? It keeps nosing my pockets. As bad as Mayor Maguire. Makes me edgy."

"She's been out there all night," Sage replied. "I'll feed her and get her back to the barn after we open gifts."

"Why didn't you just leave her at Paws and Pine," Janis asked.

"Because she was lonely," Avery explained, as if speaking to a child.

When Janis returned with her lap top she glanced over the group seated around the table. "Okay, so normally I wouldn't tell any of you about my inquiry. You're not professionals.

"On the one hand you have no clue about police business." Her eyes rolled. "But on the other hand it took all of you to solve this case. I just added up the clues, so to speak. So you deserve an explanation. Like I said, I'll be right back." She headed toward the door.

While she was gone Michael refilled the coffee mugs. "Do you think Thorny's awake?"

"He might want to hear about Janis's arrest," Meadow said. "Janis didn't say anything about Thorny. Maybe he didn't kill Baubles." The words lay in the air as Michael stood to rinse the carafe to make a fresh pot.

"And Sage was worried that Brad was involved," Meadow added. "Janis didn't mention his name either."

The front door opened and closed. "Join me in the living room, why don't you," Jets called out. "I want everyone all together. You know I hate repeating myself."

Meadow rose first, taking her coffee mug with her. Sage followed, helping her mom settle into a chair near the crackling fire. "Hey, Thorny," Sage greeted the man standing with the sleepy frown on his face.

Before Meadow could get up, Sage handed him a

cinnamon roll, pointing to a chair. "Have to keep up your strength," she told him. *Where did she get that voice of authority?* Meadow wondered. Then she felt herself flush. *Like I don't know.*

"I'm going to set my laptop right here." Jets turned the screen around so that people could see. "And then I'll play my interview from last night. Riverside police picked the killer up right after I called. Not like he was invisible, toting a trailer filled with Shetlands."

She clicked Play and continued to explain. "Justin was taking the ponies to the desert. A place called the Blue Barn Ranch. The woman who owns the ranch agreed to keep the ponies. I don't suppose she realized they were stolen. Horse people can be very trusting." She turned to face the video.

Justin Young leaning forward at the far end of a conference table. The camera angle revealed the backs of two detectives. After the usual formal introductions, the camera zeroed in on Young's face.

39

THE CHRISTMAS CONFESSION

Sage McCloud

"I killed Robert Abernathy. And I'm not sorry either. After what he did to my boy." Justin sat back in his chair, his face immobile.

"Describe the crime. Don't leave any detail out," the officer said.

The words tumbled from his lips. "Years ago, when my son was in high school, he took what they called the cinnamon challenge. He got sick. Then he did it the second time. After that, Jimmy fell into a coma. My wife Jan was so distraught that she left me.

"I spent years visiting Jimmy at the rest home. He wasted away hooked up to all those tubes. I never saw Jan again. She'd make a point to visit our son when I wasn't there.

"And then this past spring, Jimmy died. I had no one to live for after that. So I plotted my revenge." He folded his arms over his chest. "Go ahead and arrest me. Like I told you earlier, I don't need an attorney."

Jets paused the interview recording. She turned to face everyone. "A textbook confession," she said with a glint in her eye. Then she leaped to her feet to smack Thornton's hand. "That's my plate. Get your own cinnamon roll," she admonished.

Avery was the first to ask a question. "So Justin killed Baubles?"

"Robert Abernathy was Baubles's real name," Jets continued. "Thanks to Meadow's research, I put it all together. Sit back and listen." She clicked the interview back on, reaching for her last bite of roll.

Justin Young continued. "All the teens were trying the challenge. Because of that idiot, Robert Abernathy. He'd inhale cinnamon, not liquid or anything, and then all of his college pals laughed and goaded him on. It went viral on the internet, and then stupid high school kids tried it themselves. I warned my son, but like most teens, he thought he knew best. So he just went along with his pals."

Justin stopped to wipe his hand over his eyes. "Once we realized what he'd done, we took Jimmy to the ER. He had asthma, you know. He recovered but was never able to do much after that. Needed inhalers. Had to be put on oxygen numerous times. Couldn't play sports or even sing in church."

Avery sniffed loudly while Janis stopped the taped interview. "That's enough," she said. "Can't have you feeling sorry for this guy." Jets snorted, looking to Michael for support. He avoided her glance.

"Okay, it's Christmas. How about I fill in the rest in my own words."

Janis stood, holding her hands in fig leaf position in

front of her blazer. "Justin's kid tragically went into a coma after he took his second cinnamon challenge. Kinda stupid, considering all the problems the first challenge caused him.

"Then years later after his kid dies, Justin tracks down Abernathy. He wants revenge plain and simple. But Robert is now Baubles and he's ten years wiser. He'd been hiding out as a clown, so ashamed that his video harmed so many kids."

"He was probably stoned when he did those challenges," Thorny muttered. "You can do a lot of crazy stuff under the influence."

"My older brother tried that challenge. He told me no one ever got hurt. Liar," mumbled Logan.

"There were no deaths reported," Janis admitted. "That's why I was skeptical at first. Turns out Jimmy Young's death went under the radar. I didn't connect this until someone finally found out Baubles's real name." She nodded at Meadow. "Librarians make good researchers." Meadow gave her a grateful smile.

Avery spoke up. "I know the clown is dead and Justin Young killed him, but what about Sparkles? He was traumatized."

"Stop it," Jets said. "That overgrown comfort pony is just fine. He's outside munching on oats, not a care in the world. We're talking about a dead person here. Big difference."

"And a dead child," added Meadow.

"That's right, Miss Marple," Jets replied. She looked around. Then when no one else objected, she continued. "Okay, I'll tell you more. Wanted to anyway. This was an interesting case."

A bell rang from the kitchen. "Hold on." Sage stood. "I have to pull out another batch of rolls. But I'll be right back. I want to hear everything."

Jets turned her chair to face the group and then sat down right when Sage returned. "Okay, so once his kid passed away—I know, very sad," Janis held up her hand and continued, "Justin tracked down Baubles. He got a job wrangling the ponies. Abernathy had no idea who he was. He probably died not knowing."

Brad spoke from the other side of the room. He looked unusually pale. "I thought Baubles was a college guy. He could have done a lot of things besides being a clown for kids at birthday parties."

"He dropped out of Stanford," Janis explained. "People harassed him and he became depressed. He hated himself. How his impulsive behavior contributed to Jimmy Young's illness and coma."

"So get back to the part where Justin got hired by Baubles," Logan insisted.

"Justin bided his time. He worked with Baubles and the ponies for a few weeks and they came up to Lily Rock. It was then he escalated. He sent little notes to Robert to make him suffer. We found those hidden in a wooden box. And then last week, Justin knew he would find Baubles in the tent alone. I guess rope tricks require practice. So Baubles used the early morning hours before the pony rides began.

"According to his own confession, Justin walked up behind Robert and slipped the rope around his neck. When Robert dropped down unconscious, that's when Justin executed the rest of his plan."

Michael interrupted. "Justin told everyone he was having breakfast when Baubles was killed."

"Not the first time a murderer has lied about his whereabouts," muttered Jets. "The guys down the hill didn't get the time of death right. They may have been in a hurry, time of year and all. But I asked forensics to look at the details again. It turns out Baubles expired earlier, by at least an hour." She glared at Michael. "So enough interrupting. We're getting to the really gory part. You'd better brace yourselves." Jets's eyes gleamed. When no one objected, she continued.

"Like I was saying, once Baubles passed out..." Janis hesitated. She surveyed the group, her glance stopping on Avery. "If you want to plug your ears, now's the time."

Avery gave her a dart eye, daring her to continue.

Janis's voice lowered. She spoke conspiratorially, with a hushed intensity. "So Justin took a bottle of cinnamon and a metal straw and blew the dust right into Baubles's throat. It must have coated his lungs and that was that. Baubles stopped breathing and died. Just like Jimmy." Jets looked very pleased with herself, relishing everyone's shocked expression.

"Well, Merry Christmas everyone," Michael said dryly.

"Ah, come on. It's good for you," Jets retorted. "Just because everyone goes all sentimental this time of year, that doesn't mean people don't keep killing other people and being general jackasses. Someone has to clean up the mess. And I'm the woman to do it!"

"I'm never eating cinnamon again," Avery whimpered.

"Great. More for me. Got one fresh out of the oven?" Janis asked.

When no one leaped up, she leaned back in her chair. "Okay, I get it. Take a minute and then I'll sum up the arrest all nice and tidy. After that we can eat."

Meadow broke the silence. "So how did you connect the metal straw with the cinnamon?"

Jets smiled. "It took Thorny."

"What do you mean?" Thorny sat up at the sound of his name.

Jets explained. "You picked up the straw because you were in the barn that morning. And then you left it at Wrap It Up!. I guess you told someone to deliver it as my present. Someone left the package on my desk at the constabulary. Once I opened it and sniffed the cinnamon, I sent it right to the lab. Of course your fingerprints were all over the metal. But just the fact that it was covered in cinnamon dust helped me put everything together." Jets cleared her throat.

"To be completely honest, all of you had something to do with solving this case. Meadow turned me on to Baubles's real name and Justin's son. And then Sage and Brad brought the wooden box from Baubles's room to the constabulary, where I found the notes coated in cinnamon.

"And Thorny left me the straw, which was the actual murder weapon. If it wasn't for Avery and Logan, delivering it to my desk, that valuable piece of evidence would be lost. They took their job so seriously, crazy kids. And Mike..." She looked at him with a grin. "Stayed out of my way for once. Thanks."

"Thorny gave me explicit directions," Avery said. "I didn't remember in the rush last night, but he left that straw on my table and told me to wrap it and give it to Janis as a Christmas present. I thought it was kinda lame at the time."

Meadow concluded. "So we all helped, in one way or another, to solve this case."

"Like Janis said, I had nothing to do with it this year." Michael held up his hands in front of him. He didn't sound one bit disappointed.

Jets turned to him to add, "Let's face it, you were way over your head last year. It was time for you to take a crime-solving break."

"Speaking of breaks," Sage's voice came from the doorway. "The fresh rolls are out of the oven. Step into the kitchen if you're ready for more Christmas goodness."

Even Janis Jets knew when to quit. She was the first through the door. "To quote Charles Dickens," Jets reached for the roll on top, "'God bless us, every one.' Now where's my coffee?"

40

THE GAME CHANGER

Sage McCloud

Later they stood on the porch, Sage and Michael looked up at a series of fluffy clouds which drifted overhead. The cold stung Sage's cheeks. Flakes began to drift from above. She watched as they landed on the blanket that covered Sparkles's back.

"We'd better get her into the barn," Sage commented.

A smile teased at the corner of Michael's mouth. "I know. But you have to admit this is perfect. The snow. Hanging out with friends. All that baking." He looked down at her. "I can't remember how long it's been since I felt this way. I feel a certain excitement, as if something's coming our way in the new year. A game changer, if you will."

Sage nodded. "I feel excited too. It's been quite the Christmas. All of a sudden I'm following in Meadow's footsteps. She's been so odd for months. Face it, I had to step up."

"You did a good job," Michael added quickly. "And you helped me because I got to help you."

"Say more about that something around the corner," she teased.

He looked uncomfortable, at a loss for words. Then he reached into his pocket. "So true confession? She's a long-time friend of Marla's.

"Marla let me keep the photo on my phone. There's something in her face. Her eyes, the way she tilts her chin. Have a look."

Sage took his phone and stared at the screen. "She's an old friend of Marla's, you say?"

"From high school. Her name's Olivia. Olivia Greer. Marla invited her for a getaway weekend in the spring. Olivia's been having some problems of her own." Sage heard a tenderness in his voice.

She took a closer look at the photo. Her heart warmed unexpectedly. *Do I know this woman?* "She looks familiar. Like you said, something about her eyes." She handed him back the phone. "Do you think she'll show up?"

"God, I hope so." He shoved his phone back in his pocket, a wistful look in his eyes. "Don't say anything to anyone, okay? Keep it between us. By the time she gets here I'll be over it anyway."

Maybe it was the snow or maybe because they'd grown closer over the holidays, but Sage heard a new longing in Michael's voice. "You're not dating anyone?" she asked shyly.

"Not really. I've never done this before, felt this way about a photo. So don't think I'm nuts or anything. But when Marla showed me this picture, I just knew..."

"Knew what?"

"That's the thing. I'm not sure. It's a feeling." He touched his chest and then looked away.

"Meadow taught me not to discredit the heart," Sage said in a serious voice.

He looked down at the snow before gazing back at her. The longing was no longer in his voice when he spoke. "I'm going to delete that photo. Just watch me." He took one last glance. "It's the time of year, you know?" He smiled at her quizzically. Then he quickly changed the subject. "Do you mind if I come along, to walk Sparkles?"

"Not at all. I'd love your company." Sage knew better than to push a man once he'd shown you his vulnerable side. "But we'd better get a move on. Because I need to put the ham in the oven so it'll be ready for dinner. Now that I'm the new Meadow, I have work to do."

The End.

This is the conclusion of the prequel series Welcome to Lily Rock Holiday Mysteries. If you want to know more about the characters and the arrival of Olivia Greer, then Getaway Death (Book One in the Lily Rock Mystery series) is available in ebook and paperback on all book platforms.

Prologue

Overheard in Lily Rock

"I love the town of Lily Rock. Their lies are so authentic."

Fog rolled over the mountain road. Despite the poor visibility, the woman drove as if her life depended upon it.

A sharp curve to the right—her squealing tires issued a warning.

Tentatively removing one hand from the steering wheel, she kept her eyes on the road, her fingers reaching down for her windshield wipers. *Swish.* The blade on the glass moved to the left, then the right. Her gaze remained fixed on the road in front of her. Reaching over the steering wheel, she swiped with her hand at the thick condensation blocking her view from inside the car.

Veering into the next curve, she felt her stomach lurch. Brakes squealed again as the car catapulted into an unexpected second hairpin turn. Her head lolled to the right. As she came out of the curve, she pushed the button on the foggy driver's side door and rolled down the window, revealing clouds of fog.

Another vehicle rumbled behind her car, close to her bumper.

"I guess somebody's in a big hurry," she snapped to the empty car.

The window slid shut as she looked out of the front windshield to the right, then the left. No turnout lane yet. Tightness stiffened her neck as her hands began to shake on the wheel. *Stop tailgating me. Please.*

She felt the tires slip on the road, the car floating for a moment. As she slammed on the brakes, her body heaved against the seat belt, her neck and head rocking forward then back. Her stomach came up to her throat.

As her car skidded toward the cliff, she only had one thought:

I finally know how I will die.

**To continue reading,
be sure to pick up *Getaway Death*
at your favorite retailer.**

If you relate to Meadow's struggle, then you are not alone. I think we all know that the secrets we keep as well as the truths we tell all mold and shape our present and future well-being.

Writing the third and final *Welcome to Lily Rock* novella brought me great joy. Each word felt as if I were laying individual stones on a path, paving the way for Olivia Greer to make that first fateful drive up the hill to the small mountain town.

When you read further, you'll discover that Olivia will serve as a catalyst to upend the entire town of Lily Rock. Michael, Janis, Brad, Meadow, and Sage will begin their own journeys of self-discovery, solving murders along the way.

The only one who remains constant is Mayor Maguire. From day one he accompanies Olivia as her indefatigable companion. He skillfully helps navigate her path as she comes to realize that the town and its inhabitants will become her new home. As the Van Morrison song says,

Olivia will be picked right up and put back down with her feet on solid ground.

Happy Reading and Welcome to Lily Rock!
Bonnie Hardy

ABOUT THE AUTHOR

You can connect with Bonnie at
bonniehardywrites.com

Bonnie Hardy, a retired professional turned author, is celebrated for her two enthralling cozy mystery series. The first, set in the picturesque mountain town of Lily Rock, features amateur sleuth Olivia Greer, known for her uncanny ability to draw out confessions from the most unlikely people.

The second series, set in Palm Desert, features the mid-life duo mentalist Rex Redondo and his down to earth next door neighbor doula Vivienne Rose.

Inspired by Agatha Christie, Bonnie's captivating tales of mystery and community masterfully blend fast-paced whodunits with clever sleuthing.